THE DRAGON OF ROME

BY JOHN SEVEN

STONE ARCH BOOKS

a capstone imprint

The Time-Tripping Faradays
are published by Stone Arch Books
A Capstone Imprint
1710 Roe Crest Drive
North Mankato, Minnesota 56003
www.capstonepub.com

Library of Congress Cataloging-in-Publication Data
Seven, John.
    The dragon of Rome / by John Seven; illustrated by Craig Phillips.
        p. cm. -- (The time-tripping Faradays)
    Summary: In Rome during the time of Vespasian, time travelers Dawkins
and Hypatia Faraday join up with Pliny the Elder who is researching
dragons for his natural history encyclopedia, which seems like a
harmless activity until a real fire-breathing dragon attacks them.
    ISBN 978-1-4342-6029-1 (library binding) -- ISBN 978-1-4342-6439-8
(pbk.) -- ISBN 978-1-62370-012-6 (paper over board)
    1. Pliny, the Elder--Juvenile fiction. 2. Dragons--Juvenile fiction. 3. Time
travel--Juvenile fiction. 4. Adventure stories. 5. Rome--History--Flavians,
69-96--Juvenile fiction. [1. Pliny, the Elder--Fiction. 2. Dragons--Fiction.
3. Time travel--Fiction. 4. Adventure and adventurers--Fiction. 5. Science
fiction. 6. Rome--History--Flavians, 69-96--Fiction. 7. Italy--History--
Fiction.] I. Phillips, Craig, 1975- II. Title.
    PZ7.S5145Dr 2013
    813.6--dc23

                        2012051715

Cover illustration: Craig Philips

Designer: Kay Fraser

Photo-Vector Credits: Shutterstock.

Printed in China by Nordica.
0413/CA21300511
032013   007226NORDF13

FOR JANA

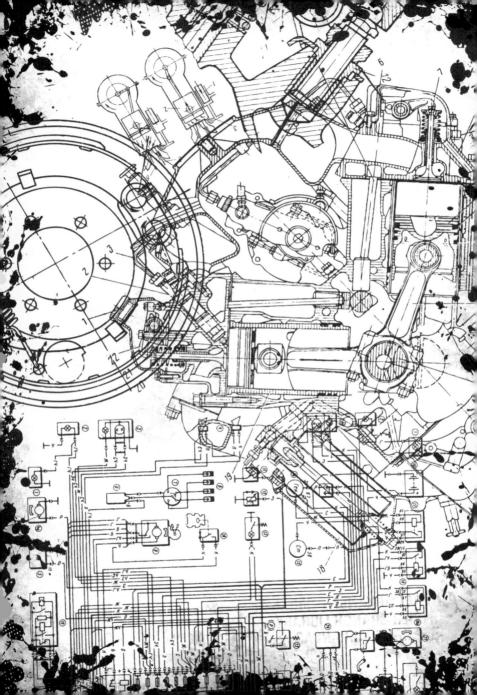

CHAPTER

1

Hype made her way through the paths in the Alvarium. No one was there. As usual. From what she could tell on the Link, everyone was hunched in their pods, playing the newest vReality PlayMod, Draggin' Dragons, which Hype was trying to avoid despite the stream in her head.

Draggin' Dragons was the biggest thing to hit PlayModCulture in ages. It was weird: the game had suddenly just been everyone's favorite one day, like it had come out of nowhere. Everyone was talking about it.

Dragons just didn't interest her much. Neither did PlayModCulture, really. Which was odd. Everyone liked vReality PlayMods. Her brother Dawk loved them and spent most of his time gaming. They made her feel weird, though, and she figured a lot of that had to do with her family business.

You see, Hype was a time traveler.

Her parents were field researchers for the Temporal History Research Division of the Cosmos Institute, currently specializing in historical footwear. Hype had seen a lot of things that her friends hadn't.

Those vReality PlayMods? They were so addictive largely because of the work people like Hype's parents did getting all the details right.

Hype had become so used to seeing it all firsthand that the vReality PlayMod just wasn't very satisfying for her.

Plus, the games never replicated smells as well as the sights and sounds. She liked the smells from the past. Even the bad ones.

Dragons calling! (Link friend)

Hype had taken to staying off the Link as much

as possible, but she was waiting to hear about her family's next assignment, so she kept it open and did her best to ignore all the chatter. Sometimes she actually envied her grandmother, who was still saddled with an old-fashioned ear-hug connection.

No time for dragons. (Hype)

You're a temporal citizen, you have all the time in the world! (Link friend)

Nothing her Link friend said could talk Hype into playing. She continued wandering through the empty Alvarium, which was basically pods clustered within a dome, and skyways connecting them.

She stopped to look out through the Alvarium and had a moment of dizziness, which was weird, because she didn't have a problem with heights. Her vision seemed messed up, and the usual gray and white walls of the pathways had become sparkled with colors.

Green. Red. Brown.

They melted in and away, in and away, pulsating, as if her brain were trying to fight them off and cling to the drab colors.

It was odd, like someone else was controlling her

NeuroNet connection, not her. But that didn't make sense. Hype didn't think that remote controlling was even possible with humans, just different bots.

Anyone else getting an override? (Hype)

I wish! Then I could concentrate on this PlayMod better! (Link friend)

Not helpful.

She closed her eyes in order to stop whatever was happening, counted to ten, and looked again—but reality had gotten worse. Or less like reality. More like a vReality Module.

She wasn't in the Alvarium anymore, but some kind of forest. Lush. Dark. Thick with trees, scattered with boulders.

She was in a vReality without giving permission to the NeuroServers. How had that happened?

Over the last couple centuries, gameplay had moved from playing on screens to PlayMods using vReality technology that streamed through the NeuroNet. Humans had begun to understand that they could experience an illusion that felt as real as anything else, and they could use that for fun and learning.

So when Hype found herself standing in the forest and hearing the trudging of a large creature, even though it was just a vReality PlayMod, it was as real to her as the Alvarium had been just moments before.

And when she smelled something smoky, she thought, *Wow, they are really getting better with the aromatic simulation in these PlayMods.*

Or maybe it was an educational module? No. Educational mods were never as well rendered as PlayMods because the developers had more fun making games for amusement, not for education.

Definitely a PlayMod with hyper-smell programming, one she hadn't agreed to sign into though she somehow got sucked in. Perhaps NeuroNet was on the blink.

Then she got a burst of scenario for the PlayMod, but didn't have a moment to consider it other than to realize she had been sucked in to play Draggin' Dragons without her permission.

She moved the scenario to her NeuroCache in case she actually did need the information, rather than playing without the help of the CartoMods that mapped this vReality's world. She'd prefer not to play at all, though.

She heard a noise behind her and quickly turned around.

A dragon.

It moved cautiously toward her through the forest, the tail deceptively sluggish. Hype knew from playing the game that it could whip her in a second. The tail might be big enough to prevent the dragons from flying, but they could still do you some damage.

It was as if the dragon itself was on the Link, because the moment she thought that, the tail went whipping toward her. She tried to leap out of the way. It was the only thing she could think quickly enough to do, but her leg was nicked by the tail and she went tumbling into a bush.

Anyone know how to win at Draggin' Dragon? (Hype)

You got the enchanted map? (Link friend)

Gotta get to the Illuminated Cave, find the dragon thorn. (Link friend)

What? (Hype)

Hype knew she could stream the info from her NeuroCache and it would all make sense to her, but she was being stubborn because she hadn't asked to be in this PlayMod.

Her only course of rebellion was refusing to take part in the action. It was just vReality—it wasn't real. She couldn't get hurt. She could afford to be stubborn about this.

Of course, it felt just the opposite as the Draggin' Dragon's tail came slamming down next to her in the bush and she had to twist out of the way, onto the muddy ground next to it.

How do I get out of here? (Hype)

Escape command is built into knots in the tree. You see it? (Link)

Hype looked around. Knots were all over the trees. There were billions of them.

Is there a particular shape I'm looking for? (Hype)

I've routed through all the NeuroChans, and finally I've found you. (Fizzbin)

Hype looked up. There was a knight in shining armor standing there, holding out his hand.

I've been trying for hours to round you up where

you're supposed to be rather than wasting time in this PlayMod. (Fizzbin)

The knight was a gaming avatar chosen by Fizzbin, her computer guardian. He didn't actually have a physical form, unless you count that of a tiny, flat computer chip known as an IntelliBoard, somewhere in the safety banks underneath the Alvarium.

Hype didn't know whether to be thankful or annoyed that Fizzbin had found her. It was nice to be rescued from the override, but he didn't have to be so stodgy about it.

She should be used to it by now. It was basically Fizzbin's job to oversee Hype and her brother, Dawk. It became his job after they had caused trouble while marching with Hannibal and his Carthaginian army. Hype got it. She knew they'd messed up. But she still felt the way Fizzbin oversaw her and her brother to be an overreaction on the part of the Chancellor.

Sure, the Chancellor was in charge of almost everything in the Alvarium and the Cosmos Institute, since he was the head of the Ruling Cluster. But he didn't have to be in charge of Hype. She could take care of herself.

It was probably a good thing that Fizzbin was here now, though.

She grasped Fizzbin's hand—or, rather, the heavy gauntlet that covered the virtual hand he had within this PlayMod—and began to pull herself up. She didn't really expect that the Draggin' Dragon, at that exact moment, would decide to go swinging the tail again. It began whomping heavily toward Fizzbin.

Hype did the worst thing possible—she cowered. That was not how you got through a PlayMod, and the level would probably start over if she and Fizzbin were crushed.

But maybe that was a plus. Maybe that would give them time to find an escape command before the Draggin' Dragon came back.

But then the unexpected happened. Fizzbin held up his other arm and stopped the dangerous tail cold in the air.

How did you do that? (Hype)

It's merely part of the conversation I am having with

another IntelliBoard, the one that runs this PlayMod. I'm trying to get it to put some gameplay rules on override so we can get you out of here. I am informed that the customary way to defeat the dragon is to climb onto the tail while it is in motion, shimmy up its back, and strike it at a certain spot there with the side of your hand. That paralyzes it. Would you like to try? (Fizzbin)

No. Can you just ask where an escape command is? I've looked at all these knots on the trees and I can't find one. (Hype)

Unnecessary. An escape code has been provided to me. See you on the other side. (Fizzbin)

The vReality disappeared faster than it had taken over, and Hype felt disoriented and groggy, like she was coming out of a coma. Patches of light zoomed to her eyes and she blinked to bring reality into focus.

When she did, she didn't feel much better. The first thing she saw was her parents and her brother gathered around her and staring down at her as she lay on a couch.

"Fizzbin found you," Dad said. "Not the best time to enter a PlayMod."

"When we get back from ancient Rome," Mom said, "I'm afraid you're going to find yourself in serious trouble."

CHAPTER

2

Dawk stared out from the window of the family's quarters and looked out at ancient Rome. It wasn't so unlike the Alvarium, just with simpler materials and actual open space. Oh, and crowds of people moving around.

When he was younger, Dawk would have preferred the familiar comfort of any vReality, PlayMod or educational mod, to whatever era they were in. Now, though, he was finding himself more interested in his immediate surroundings than in his perceived ones, and having Fizzbin constantly monitoring him on the Link made him less likely to stream nonsense at his friends.

He had become more disciplined in his NeuroNet activities, and especially appreciative of some distance from them after a recent incident in seventeenth-century Prague that had left him offline for a period of time. There, he and Hype had to think on their feet, no diversion, no help. It turned out that it was way better than a PlayMod.

Mom and Dad had gotten to work on their footwear research as soon as they had arrived in 75 AD. They were preparing for a meeting with the Roman Emperor and trying to decide what their first order of business should be.

"There are a lot more kinds of shoes for Romans than I thought," Dad said.

"There's a lot more to Rome than sandals," Mom agreed. "I love the cat boots some of the soldiers wear."

"Oh, I know," Hype said. "If women could wear short tunics, that would be an excellent outfit together."

"That could never happen here," Mom said,

"and time travelers don't want to stand out, so I don't advise you adopt that style either."

◦◎ ❖ ◎◦

As Hype and Dawk walked through Rome, Fizzbin provided an ongoing narration for anything they saw, thanks to his tiny OpBot, which sped up ahead and streamed all sights back through the temporal-chan of the NeuroNet. The scene on the streets was busy, with Roman citizens zooming every which way as if they all had something very important to do and couldn't take the time for simple courtesy.

This is one of the forums, the center of social and political life for Romans. Beware of politicians and thieves, though it is difficult to tell the difference between them. (Fizzbin)

The passage through the forum was flanked by stalls that sold anything you could think of. It seemed to Dawk that every other building was a temple. Columns and statues galore.

But as they moved further, one massive construct

in the distance didn't look like it had a religious purpose.

Hype pointed. "What's that?"

The Flavian Amphitheater. It will later be better known as the Colosseum. We will soon arrive there. (Fizzbin)

There was a crowd to their left, and it appeared some sort of pomp was going on. Hype motioned for Dawk to follow her over to take a closer look. Walking in the middle of all the people was a serious-looking man with a noble nose. The expression on his face was one of strain, like he had been injured. But he laughed when someone spoke to him.

Dawk ran a facial recognition search through NeuroNet and came up with the current Caesar.

"That's Vespasian," he said. "This guy runs all of this. Actually, in the ancient world, he runs almost everything there is, at least in this hemisphere."

"He's not very fancy for an emperor," Hype said, gazing at the man.

An old soldier not inclined to show off. What they used to call a man of action in the days when wars were fought. (Fizzbin)

"Hey, look, it's Mom and Dad!" Dawk said, pointing.

They were in the background of the crowd that was gathering and pushing toward Vespasian, looking sullen and uncomfortable.

Dawk wasn't sure what to think.

Did his parents' facial expressions mean the mission was not going very well? And what did that mean when you were sent to study footwear in Rome?

Oh, gee, they look grumpy. I'm not going there, let's keep moving. (Dawk)

They continued through the pathways of the forum. As they got closer to the Colosseum, it slowly began to overtake the scenery in front of them. It seemed like there were thousands of people working on it. Some were building, while others hauled huge columns and marble statues on wooden trolleys and hoisted them onto the workplace.

"It's a miracle of engineering, but don't try to sleep late if your quarters are anywhere nearby," came a voice.

Dawk and Hype both turned around to see an older gentleman standing behind them. He was smiling warmly despite the crankiness of his statement.

"The slaves make a racket," the man added. "Far more than seems likely for what they're building here. I've a mind to go in and inspect the work myself. Especially in the middle of the night, when it just becomes unbearable. Are you students? Or gawkers?"

"Just gawkers," Hype said with a wide smile. "Though we could become students at the drop of a hat."

"Ah, but if you were a freed slave, you would not want to drop your hat, for the pileus is proof of your freedom," the man said. He chortled.

That was an example of hilarious upper-class Roman humor. I suggest you laugh. (Fizzbin)

Dawk and Hype laughed right away, even though they didn't really understand the joke at all.

What's a pileus? (Dawk)

It's a sort of fez that freed slaves wore to prove they were free. (Fizzbin)

If I had known that, I wouldn't have laughed. (Dawk)

Bad jokes are just another unavoidable part of time travel. (Hype)

CHAPTER

3

One of the pitfalls of being a time traveler was that people were always laughing about things that made no sense to you. One time they had gone to ancient Mesopotamia. Everyone was cracking up about fish and towers and eye gouging, and Dawk and Hype just looked on, dumbfounded.

You might wish to change the subject to the matter at hand. You could always mention the tones of Greek architecture within the Colosseum's design. (Fizzbin)

"I can't believe how Greek the Colosseum looks," Dawk said.

The man looked at Dawk and frowned.

"What my brother means," Hype interrupted, "is that the design obviously references Greek design and functions as a link through history between our two enlightened societies."

Dawk accessed NeuroPedia quickly. He scanned the entry. Stonemasons . . . arches . . . blah, blah, blah . . . concrete. Concrete?

Concrete!

"It's really amazing, this new substance, concrete," Dawk said. "So much more exciting than limestone."

He streamed the information through the Link to Hype, who picked it up quickly.

"Oh, yes, I hope it's as resilient as they predict," Hype said. "It could mean the Amphitheatrum Flavium will stand for the rest of history."

Dawk was sure they were coming off as truly Roman to this old guy.

"Do you know much of the latest advances?" the man asked.

"We like to keep up with, um, the current knowledge," Hype said.

"And the natural world? Do you know much about the natural world?"

"Of course. We follow everything!" Dawk said.

"Well, if you are looking for sponsorship, I always have need of researchers in my encyclopedias," the old man said. "Might I introduce myself? My name is Pliny. I work in several capacities for the Emperor Vespasian, but when I work for myself, which is daily, it is to compile my Natural Histories. You seem bright enough. Would that interest you?"

I don't know about this. (Dawk)

It's something to do when we're not taking in great architecture. (Hype)

It will also keep you out of trouble. (Fizzbin)

"We'd love to," Hype said.

"Very good," the man said. "Shall we say tomorrow, midday? My home is just over there. Just observe where the clanking becomes loudest and you have found me. I currently have many interesting channels of pursuit, and your help will only make my Natural Histories that much better. Perhaps you will bring further knowledge of hedgehogs, for instance."

He began to wander off. "I am off to the dedication of the Temple of Peace; the Emperor expects me. But tomorrow, we look for dragons!"

As the man walked away, Dawk immediately searched NeuroPedia for the official word on dragons.

Mythological.

I could have told you that. (Fizzbin)

CHAPTER

4

Dinner that night was mutton, beets, and bread, with cups of diluted wine—that was the way the Romans preferred it—and garnished with olives, olive relish, and olive oil to dip the bread in. Olive bread. It was the sort of meal that would probably make a NutroFabricator from Dawk and Hype's time explode. Food-synthesis machines were very delicate instruments.

Dawk and Hype had been warned that they'd better get used to olives, because there were a lot of them floating around the Roman Empire and landing on dinner plates when you least expected them. Dawk made it a personal rule to never expect them.

"Our task here is harder than we thought," Dad said. "Apparently, the Emperor hasn't got much interest in footwear. In fact, he hates footwear."

"That sounds a little silly, Dad," Hype said.

"Oh, no," Mom said, "I was there and witnessed the whole thing. We had just been given an audience with the Emperor where we were about to declare our area of expertise, but when we walked in, he was berating a bunch of Roman sailors who were traveling on land and were asking for a shoe allowance in the ranks."

"He told them no, point-blank," Dad said, "and told them they should just go barefoot from now on. What could they say to that?"

"The man is anti-shoe!" Mom said.

"I'm sure there must be more to this than the Emperor hating shoes," Hype said.

"Roman Emperors are very weird, dear," Mom said. "They have very weird views and do weird things. If you told me that one of them had it in for hats and went on a tirade about them, it wouldn't surprise me, not one bit."

"Do they hate hats in this era?" Dawk asked.

"You know what I mean," Mom said.

"So what did you end up doing?" asked Hype.

"What could we do?" said Dad, shrugging. "We complimented him on the Temple of Peace and told him it was the finest collection of art looted from victims of war that we had ever seen."

To be fair, it was Emperor Nero who stole the works of art, not Emperor Vespasian. Letting the Romans see the art is his way of making up for Nero stealing them from Judea. (Fizzbin)

"What did I tell you?" Mom said. "Weird. Anyway, what did you two do today?"

"We met Pliny the Elder," Hype said.

"I hope he's not as shifty as that alchemist you hung around with in Prague," Dad muttered.

"Pliny is a legend," Hype protested. "He practically invented the encyclopedia."

"Yeah, without him, we probably wouldn't even have a NeuroPedia," Dawk said. "No one would have thought of it."

Dawk and Hype were invited to study under Pliny in the capacity of research assistants helping to compile his seminal works of natural history. (Fizzbin)

"We'll just be helping him fact-check things about bugs and rocks," Dawk said.

"He's particularly interested in anything we might know about hedgehogs," Hype said.

"And do you know what a hedgehog is?" Mom asked.

Dawk and Hype looked at each other. "Not yet," Hype admitted.

∗

The next day, Dawk and Hype took their time getting out of bed, despite the constant chattering from Fizzbin. They were both awake, but lounging until it was time to leave for Pliny's, comfortable and expecting a busy day.

It is a great responsibility to assist Pliny. The information you gather for his encyclopedia will affect the world for centuries. (Fizzbin)

It will be a bad idea to lie to him or make things

up. You must follow his example of careful observation. (Fizzbin)

And in the areas that he happens to get it wrong— for instance, I suggest you look further into some of the man's unusual ideas about hedgehogs—it would be good form to allow him to continue getting these facts wrong. After all, someone at a later date will be inspired by Pliny to further study the matter, like hedgehogs, and correct that information for future researchers. (Fizzbin)

"I still don't know what a hedgehog is," Hype mumbled. "The etymology suggests some kind of pig, though."

Dawk started to climb out of bed. It was just as well that he couldn't go back to sleep. Even though he had managed to ignore Fizzbin entirely, his Link messages from twenty-fifth-century friends had begun to pile up so high that it alerted his brain. This began to allow in trickles of his friends chatting to each other about a round of Quantum Car Chase. That was a very confusing PlayMod to enter, largely thanks to its principle of Automobile Uncertainty and the scenario of driving a vehicle that was actually two vehicles and not knowing which vehicle you were actually in and where it was actually going. Very challenging.

He stumbled into the dining area of their quarters, where Mom and Dad were sitting at a table. They were reading the morning *Acta Diurna*, a news sheet that was posted around the capital city and offered as much information about gladiatorial combat as you could stand.

"What's for breakfast?" Dawk asked, trying to avoid the steady flow of incomprehensible exclamations and snarky quips that were now exploding through the NeuroChan that had gotten access to him. "I hope not olives again."

But that was exactly what was for breakfast, along with warm goat's milk. Dawk and Hype silently munched the food, each hoping that their family's next assignment was for a time with better food. They had heard so much about the twenty-first century and its cuisine, for instance, but had never been sent there. Apparently, all the food was frozen into bricks and thawed out for meals. Everything had cheese in it, and some kind of mysterious syrup made out of corn. It all sounded very curious.

After forcing down the unappealing Roman breakfast, they both took to the streets with Fizzbin's OpBot nearby. The OpBot zoomed around the passersby, invisible thanks to its tiny visual cortex shell that guided what the eyes of the Romans could see.

"What do you suppose Pliny will have us do first?" Hype asked.

"Hopefully work on a lengthy entry about the rich and delicious foods of the Caesars," Dawk said. "With samples for research."

CHAPTER 5

When they got to Pliny's, he already had guests. At first, it seemed like the men were arguing, but then Dawk and Hype realized that were just trying to talk over the noise of the Colosseum construction.

"This is my patron, Titus, and his brother, Domitian," Pliny said with a smile.

Both men gave Dawk and Hype an "of course, we know that you know who we are" kind of smirk, but neither Dawk nor Hype had a clue who the men were.

They watched as Fizzbin's OpBot stealthily hovered close to the men in order to cross-reference facial recognition on the NeuroNet.

"You must be the research assistants Pliny has been blathering on about this morning," said Titus, the one with the chubby, calm face.

"The boy looks as dull as last year's hatchet," said the other one, Domitian, who had a protruding chin. "I imagine he won't be able to tell a goat from a pig."

"Then it's just as well that I don't need a goat and pig differentiated," Pliny said, "as I am already well aware of what makes a goat a goat, and a pig a pig."

"Perhaps farm beasts are not their field of expertise," Titus said. "As Pliny's patron, I not only see that he is well funded, but also well stocked with examples of natural mysteries. I was just bringing him this treasure to look at. Perhaps it might mean something to you." He held out something and offered it over to Dawk and Hype.

"Oh, not this bit of tree bark again," sneered Domitian. "It's boring, Titus."

Hype took it and looked at it closely. It was dirty green and looked like a scale from an animal— something you might find on a turtle or an armadillo, both of which Hype had seen in her travels—but tougher. More fierce.

I will have the OpBot scan for analysis, but I am still working on facial recognition and cannot provide you with the information about this strange article until that function is completed. (Fizzbin)

It seemed to Hype that an IntelliBoard like Fizzbin should be able to do at least a million things at once, but she realized that personality engineering used up all the nanocircuits and slowed calculations and functions.

For all the data sacrifice, it wasn't as if Fizzbin was that full of personality.

"I'd say it's a creature's scale," Hype said.

"Me, too," Dawk said. "I mean, that's what I immediately thought, too."

Titus laughed. "Oh, you've got some keen ones with you now, Pliny!" he said. "This is, in fact, the scale of a dragon. I procured it today after having witnessed one flying to the north of the city."

"How lucky, it fell directly into his hands!" said Pliny, beaming.

"Just missing his head by this much," added Domitian.

"A dragon here?" said Hype. "I thought they were only in the north, in Germany and beyond."

That information was courtesy of the CartoMod for Draggin' Dragons, which sat in her NeuroCache just waiting for the moment when a map of dragons habitats would be useful. That moment had now come and passed.

"I think they must be migrating," Titus said. "Pliny has other ideas."

Domitian rolled his eyes. "Father is expecting us, Titus," he said. "We have an Empire to help administer. It can't be all tree bark and dragon scales and German daydreams." Then he absentmindedly waved and wandered outside.

"Good luck on your first day with Pliny," Titus said.

Then he left, too, and Dawk and Hype were alone with their new Roman mentor

"This way!" Pliny said.

He led them through his home to a small study.

I have results galore for you. Facial recognition files place Titus and Domitian as the sons of Emperor Vespasian. Titus will rule Rome in four years, while Domitian will take over in six years from the current time. Titus is said to have been a graceful leader. Domitian was just another Roman monster. (Fizzbin)

Well, that was depressing. Hype didn't want to ask why Titus stopped being Emperor because she had a feeling she knew why already. It had something to do with his horrible brother.

And the dragon's scale? Petrified wood? (Hype)

Bone and keratin. Organic matter. I don't know if it belongs to a dragon, since there is no historical record of them, but it belongs to some creature I cannot currently identify. (Fizzbin)

I think it might belong to a goat. Or a pig. I'm not really sure, though. (Dawk)

CHAPTER 6

That's a Westphalian Whomper! (Link friend)

The tail's a killer. (Link friend)

Hype had let the Link stream in for a moment. She wasn't sure why. She shifted back to privacy. Maybe she'd wanted some validation that this wasn't all a dream—or worse, another PlayMod. But everyone was streaming about Draggin' Dragons, and here she was, about to go hunting a dragon. Would it turn out to be a Westphalian Whomper? Was she just part of the NeuroNet vReality without realizing it?

She hoped not. That would mean that Pliny's study wasn't real, and that would be awful. The room was filled with all sorts of specimens—animal, vegetable, and mineral—along with drawings, tiny sculptures, and piles of scrolls. It wasn't so much messy as it was busy, and that was exactly how Hype imagined it would look if she were to peek inside Pliny's mind.

"Now, over here is much of my latest information on birds," Pliny said, "which I think might come in handy when investigating dragons, since they are both creatures of the air."

He laughed and pulled up a sketch. "Though not all birds take to the skies. For instance, this ostrich does just the opposite—it shoves its head into the ground."

I'm sorry, I cannot let that go. I know what I told you earlier but just a glance at the NeuroBanks on ostriches reveals that to be a myth, largely perpetrated by Pliny, and though our directive is surely to avoid changing the course of history, I cannot fathom how correcting one simple fact about ostriches could possibly— (Fizzbin)

"Wow, those birds sound dumb," said Dawk.

"I wouldn't want one leading me into battle against barbarian hordes," Pliny said, laughing. "A raven, though, I would trust. Some ravens are known to have adopted the human tongue and have been given funerals that would rival those in the highest levels of state. But we are here for dragons!"

He pulled out several scrolls and handed them to Dawk and Hype. "You might want to acquaint yourself with what I have gathered so far," Pliny told them. "The information you will find here has allowed me to postulate why dragons might be descending on Rome. For instance, eagles."

Dawk and Hype said nothing. What could they say?

"Eagles and dragons are sworn enemies," Pliny went on. "Most battles end with them plummeting to equal doom! But what if by some circumstance, the eagles were wiped out at a greater rate than the dragons? The dragons, like any warrior, would tire of lazing around and begin looking for trouble in lands far and wide. I have dispatched several agents north to look into the eagle count in some of the lands where dragons typically reside."

"So we need to help you figure that out once and for all?" asked Hype.

"No, no, no," said Pliny, "I just need you to help with simple observation. My eyes are not what they used to be. If I spot a dragon I can see its form, but it's the more intense descriptions that escape me. I can't see well enough to create a description of its epidermis, of its gait, of the movement of wings, of limbs, of tail gestures. You get the idea."

"So you don't want us to help you discover the dragon's origins?" Dawk asked.

"I'll proclaim that to be a side interest to the main purpose of the entry into the encyclopedia," Pliny told him. "Once we have our statistics down, we will certainly have descriptions of many species of dragons, and we can compare and contrast what we observe. In any case, we need to wait for the eagle counts in order to have a second point in our theory. This could take time."

❧ ❖ ☙

Walking through Rome later, Dawk and Hype

followed Pliny further past the Colosseum than they had been before. There, the crowds became smaller and smaller. Soon enough, the glories of Rome were behind them and they were walking on country roads.

"Alongside olives, walking is one of the purest pleasures of the world!" Pliny said, beaming.

Perhaps he was right, at least about the walking part, but it was hard for Dawk and Hype to enjoy it. It wasn't long before their feet were killing them.

And try complaining about that on the Link. Dawk did. Everyone was too busy playing Draggin' Dragons to respond.

The Roman roads were helpful, though. They were the best in the ancient world and helped make the hike smooth. Roads were one of the Romans' greatest achievements—that, and putting olives into every single meal. But, Dawk thought, it would have been nice to have horses for their travel along those Roman roads.

Every once in a while, a chariot or a merchant with a cart of goods would pass by, and Pliny would ask, simply, "Spotted any dragons today?"

Except for the one jolly man who replied that he had not and added, "Nor have I striped any today," all others just said, "Not today."

"It's a lovely day for dragon hunting," Hype commented after they'd been walking for a couple of hours.

"Hunting?" replied Pliny. "We are not dragon hunting. We are dragon watching. Observing. To hunt is to stop something in its tracks. That's fine for survival, but an affront to education."

The hikers were now surrounded by fields on the edge of a thick forest. Pliny led Dawk and Hype off the road and into the high grass.

"This is where I saw it," Pliny told them. "The dragon."

"You saw a dragon too?" Hype asked.

"My eyes are not as good as Titus's," Pliny said. "But yes, I too saw one of the beasts. At first I thought it was from India, since it was far too big for the Ethiopian variety, but it was heading toward Rome, which places its origin in the direction opposite India."

Pliny traced the dragon's previous flight pattern

with his finger. "I eventually settled on the thought that it could be the dragon of Ladon," he said.

He's talking about a mythical dragon in a story about the Garden of Hesperides. It guarded the golden apples for the goddess queen Juno and fought Hercules. (Fizzbin)

The Hercules PlayMod is awful. There's one level where you actually have to clean out horse stables. I couldn't stand it. (Dawk)

"There's plenty of argument whether the stories of Ladon are true," Pliny explained, "or how his own story actually ended. Some say Hercules slayed him. If this was Ladon I saw in the sky, it would be a major discovery in history, perhaps even a clue to the location of the garden."

Pliny began feeling around in the sack he carried. "I've packed some olives and bread," he said. "Shall we have some respite here for the moment, look to the skies, and wait patiently?"

Olives? Ugh. I hope this is a fast dragon. (Dawk)

Just stuff your face with the bread like you usually do. (Hype)

They all sat down in the field. The break gave Pliny an opportunity to talk and talk and talk, focusing on every bit of knowledge he had gathered. Much of it was correct. Some of it was not quite there, but almost. And then there were all the things that made no sense whatsoever, like his assertion that because the brain was so wet, it was influenced by the moon.

"Just like the tides," Pliny lamented. "With the full moon comes madness."

This man is implying that the moon affects the human brain as it does the waves, which means he thinks the moon is what makes the brain all wavy. Total nonsense. (Fizzbin)

You don't like this guy, do you? (Dawk)

I should clarify. I mean physically wavy. Or perhaps wobbly or wiggly are the more appropriate terms. The man is claiming because of water in the brain, a full moon drives humans mad by making their brains wobble and wiggle like the tides of the ocean. I believe his brain is wobbling and wiggling like the tides of the ocean, that's almost for certain. (Fizzbin)

Dawk and Hype both ignored Fizzbin. They kept looking at the sky, listening to Pliny ramble on. Pliny went on about several kinds of fish and was onto the intricacies of elephant behavior when a splotch appeared in the sky. The splotch grew larger by the moment until movement could be seen on either side of its center.

Dawk pointed.

Pliny nodded. "Come, let's find a better vantage point than the ground."

They all got up and walked toward the part of the sky that the dragon was currently flying in.

"Remember, I need your sharp eyes and minds," Pliny said. "Observe everything."

Is that really a dragon? (Dawk)

Dragons don't exist. Right, Fizzbin? (Hype)

Based on these visual readings and on the previous sample of the scale, I would say that you are witnessing an actual dragon. That is, of course, impossible, and we shall begin the work of figuring out what you are really looking at. (Fizzbin)

Aren't you supposed to keep us out of trouble? (Hype)

There is no trouble to be found in learning to identify species of flying creatures. (Fizzbin)

The dragon flew closer and closer to where Dawk, Hype, and Pliny stood. And it flew fast.

Judging from the estimated speed, the estimated distance, and the estimated height, I expect the creature will pound into your current location in less than ten seconds. (Fizzbin)

Fizzbin was right. The creature came screeching down to the earth. It flew so close that they ducked down on the ground for cover.

"Well, I've never seen a dragon engage with a human," Pliny said.

"Did it just attack us?" Hype asked.

My understanding of dragon myths leads me to believe an attack would involve fire. That was just a dramatic swoop. Perhaps it wanted a closer look at you three. (Fizzbin)

Maybe it was trying to steal Dawk's olives. (Hype)

"I don't know if he was engaging with us," Dawk said. "He didn't seem to notice us."

"I just know it was really big," Hype said.

OpBot readings pinpoint it at ninety feet long. There's nothing in the twenty-fifth century to compare that to, since space is so precious in the Alvarium. (Fizzbin)

The dragon had circled back and was heading again toward the three. "Run!" Hype yelled.

"To the forest!" Dawk added. He and his sister helped Pliny struggle back to his feet.

"Maybe the cover of the trees will protect us from him," Dawk said.

The three ran and made it into the forest well ahead of the dragon. Hype looked back. Through the trees, she could see it was still coming fast. "Go deeper into the woods!" she said. But before they could run, the dragon glided up over the forest with its mouth opened, directing a rain of fire onto the trees. For a brief moment, everything was red.

And then it was on fire.

Dawk and Pliny seemed stunned. Hype pushed them back out of the woods—it was the only safe direction. Little bits of fire were dropping from the tops of the trees and igniting the forest floor. This created a path of flame that chased the three from behind until they finally outran the blaze, reaching the open-air field and leaving the flames behind in the forest, where they were still going strong.

"The fire will probably spread to the field and do some damage," Hype said. "We should get to the road and get out of here."

"I'm just terribly upset about the fire," Pliny said. "It prevented a clear view of the creature's retreat. Now we shall not know exactly where it goes, where its lair is."

On the contrary, the dragon—or whatever it is—is circling back and hitting the horizon in the west. You can tell Pliny that the dragon's lair is somewhere on the outskirts of Rome. (Fizzbin)

The OpBot went whirring into the distance. Fizzbin streamed the aerial footage to Dawk and Hype.

Do you see that? (Hype)

What? (Dawk)

That opening in the ground. (Hype)

Good eyes, Hypatia. That's where the dragon—or whatever it is—went. Now it is just a matter of looking into what is in the cave, and why a dragon—or whatever it is—has settled so close to a populated area like Rome. (Fizzbin)

"Actually, Pliny, I was paying attention, just like you asked," Hype said. "And I think you're going to find this a bit surprising."

CHAPTER

7

While Dawk and Hype were being attacked by an actual real dragon—real as in really there flying in the sky, anyhow—the Link had been streaming with excitement over an expansion to Draggin' Dragons that added a new species of dragon.

This seemed silly to Hype. Like being burned to a crisp was any different from one fake species of the monster to another. They had felt the real heat. It wouldn't matter who was doing the charring.

Normal kids from the twenty-fifth century would probably choose to sit around and stream in the new expansion of Draggin' Dragons and stay out of trouble. Not Dawk and Hype. They planned to go find more dragons.

And so the next morning, Dawk, Hype, and Pliny were once again walking to the outskirts of Rome.

You think we're going to have to eat olives for lunch again? (Dawk)

Could be worse. (Hype)

Yes, he could have garum sauce to dip the olives in. (Fizzbin)

Hype did a quick NeuroPedia search and immediately wished she hadn't. Garum sauce was made from rotting fish. Hopefully Dawk didn't make the same mistake she did. He looked a little green, though, so he had probably looked it up, too.

"Once we find the dragon, I suggest we also keep our eyes peeled for the biggest boulders to hide behind," Pliny said. "I suppose we should have brought shields."

He held out a small bowl filled with olives. "Peckish?"

Dawk shook his head, but Hype took one and

popped it in her mouth. "I wonder if there's a way to put out the fire in a dragon," she said. "If only there was a way to pump water out of the aqueducts."

"Ah, a well-positioned siphon would put out the blaze in the creature's belly," mused Pliny. "I have often wondered the source of the dragon's fire. Is it actually in the torso? In the chest and lungs? Is it perhaps in the throat? Of all the creatures that I have studied, I think I should most like to dissect a dragon and uncover the source of its fury. Perhaps it is the same configuration in their bodies as in volcanoes—that's another fiery beast I'd like to get a closer look at."

Hype sighed. "If I were you," she said, "I'd steer clear of volcanoes."

When they got to the cave entrance, they waited outside for a minute, taking it in silently. Pliny stepped forward and tried to see inside, but it was very dark inside.

"You'd think a dragon's lair would be better lit," Pliny muttered. "Oh, well, ever onward into the abyss."

Dawk grabbed the old man's shoulder. "Not you," he said.

"Nonsense!" Pliny barked.

"Do you want to find out about what's in there?" asked Hype. "Do you want to hear about our observations and learn something, or do you want us to spend all our time helping you get over all the craggy rocks you're going to stumble over in the darkness?"

"Well, perhaps I'm not as young as I once was," Pliny admitted. He frowned. "You're very pushy, for assistants."

"We're not pushy, we're concerned," Hype responded.

Pliny held out his bowl. "Here, take some olives to keep nourishment and keep your nerve."

"No, thanks." Dawk shook his head, smiled, and walked in the cave with Hype.

You'll do anything to avoid olives. (Hype)

True. (Dawk)

I will provide some lighting once you are beyond Pliny's vision. (Fizzbin)

Dawk and Hype moved cautiously inward. The

bit of light streaming in from the entrance showed a high ceiling of stone gray, with some hanging bits dripping down to the damp ground. It was huge inside. That made sense, since it apparently housed a dragon. But the room was shaped like an arch and that made it feel strangely confining.

When the entrance was just a slight wisp of light, and Pliny no longer registered as a shadow in the middle of it, the OpBot moved downward near Dawk and Hype's feet. It hovered along with its light aimed downward to the floor of the cave.

To keep you from tripping. (Fizzbin)

Just be glad you don't have feet. (Dawk)

Hype focused on the ground. You never knew what you might find in ancient Rome, in a cave, in the dark. Mostly she just saw pebbles and bugs, but she was holding out for something a little more amazing.

It was because she was the only one really paying attention that Dawk went tumbling down as he made contact with something scaly, tubular, and enormous.

Is that the dragon's tail? (Hype)

Yes. (Fizzbin)

Hype froze, waiting for a blast of fire to come out of the pitch black and char them.

But there was nothing.

Hype reached down and touched the tail. It was cold.

Is it dead? (Hype)

Scanning has commenced. (Fizzbin)

What's that flickering? (Dawk)

It was fire.

We must have woken it up. Hide! (Hype)

She cowered behind a boulder, hoping that it would shield her from the dragon's fury.

Dawk, are you safe? (Hype)

I guess so. (Dawk)

I will try to keep you aware of each other's placement as the dragon reacts. (Fizzbin)

They waited.

It sure does take its time waking up. (Dawk)

They kept waiting.

Nothing happened.

Hype realized that she should hear the dragon's body moving, scraping against the cave floor or something. But there was no sound other than some slight taps that sounded nothing like dragon slither, but were certainly getting louder.

The flicker of the fire was still evident on the cave walls. The light was getting closer.

Then they heard a man's voice.

"Do you understand what Antevorta told us?"

The voice came from the direction of the faint flicker.

"It is just a slight matter of resuscitation that is common in all dragons."

That was another voice.

"I never knew that," the first voice said.

"The igniter is along the spine. It's central to the workings of a dragon."

"What? The fire?"

"Yes, the fire," the second voice said. "If it flickers and goes out, the dragon slumps. You need to get it going again. It's just nature. Come, let's find the igniter."

The light got closer, eventually shining down on the massive dragon and making clearer the Romans who were carrying the torch. The older men were gladiator types. They were studying the dragon as they approached it.

Who are they? (Hype)

I can't process their facial patterns enough to run them through the facial recognition channels. (Fizzbin)

They came from the other side of the cave. (Dawk)

So? (Hype)

So that means there are two ends to this cave. Do caves usually have two ends? (Dawk)

Two ends make it more of a tunnel. I'm going in farther. (Hype)

I have safety concerns about that. (Fizzbin)

Those two guys seem okay to me, and I'd just be going wherever they came from. (Hype)

A bug just flew into my mouth. Watch out for that. (Dawk)

Hype slowly rose from her hiding spot behind the boulder. She couldn't see much of anything, so she moved carefully. The two men were still talking, preoccupied by feeling around for the igniter they had been talking about.

Hype was far enough away from their firelight that if she was careful, it wouldn't be hard to slink past them and move deeper into the cave to find out what was at the other end.

Once she got past them, she began to walk faster. But she had to be careful not to go so fast that if she hit a rock she would break a toe or go tumbling or anything.

"That's it!" came one of the voices. "I'm feeling a resuscitation."

Then she heard thumping, along with a hiss so loud that it bounced around in her ears and didn't go away even when she covered them.

It's up! Run, Hype! (Dawk)

She ran, but the furious noise from behind was so loud that it echoed in her head. She found herself toppling over from the force of the roar and the wind created by something huge flying over her.

The dragon. It was back in the air and now flying deeper into the tunnel.

Hype lay still on the ground. She had knocked her head and was disoriented and the Link was feeding through her brain without stopping, and she couldn't turn it off.

If Dawk or Fizzbin were trying to say anything

to her, they were lost in a wave of gibberish about the hot PlayMod of the day.

She slowly pulled herself up on her knees and then stood up. When she walked, her knee hurt. It wasn't bad enough to worry about, but she definitely noticed it. She couldn't see ahead very well, but moved as quickly as she could anyhow in order to stay ahead of the two men. They had now started walking back to the other end of the tunnel, where Hype was headed.

The Link still streamed on, but Hype did her best to ignore it. She was too busy trying to follow that dragon, even if she couldn't quite see where she was going.

CHAPTER

8

As Hype walked through the entire length of the cave, her limp went away and her brain became less addled. That allowed her to block out much of the Link, which had been streaming in like a dam had broken. Every once in a while, Dawk or Fizzbin checked in with her to ask her where she was. She could only answer: in a dark cave.

But now it looked like she had finally reached the end of the line, well ahead of the two gladiators. The cave led to a three-sided chamber formed by concrete and lined with torches. The dragon was resting in it. Well, resting wasn't quite the word. The dragon was there, and it was chained up—so it wasn't moving much. It just flailed angrily as wisps of smoke and fire nervously spurted out of its nasal and throat passages.

Hype almost felt sorry for it.

She moved closer to get a look at the beast. It was definitely awake. It looked like a majestic creature, but only as long as it couldn't go on the attack.

On one side of the chamber was an iron gate. It looked to Hype as though the dragon was chained in such a way that it couldn't reach the gate, so she figured that was her best bet to move forward. She started to hear echoes of voices behind her and caught the faint flicker of fire, which made her get on the move toward the door. She had to stay ahead of the gladiators.

As long as she didn't get charred to a crisp by dragon breath, she would be fine.

As she moved through the gate, the dragon seemed to notice her. But it wasn't snapping at her or trying to reach her with a claw or its tail or anything. A shower of fire didn't even seem likely. The dragon appeared to be disinterested in her.

She didn't look back once she got through. She was too curious to see what was on the other side. Someone seemed to be keeping a pet dragon, but why anyone would do that and where they would grab a dragon was entirely a mystery just waiting to be solved.

Have you seen anything yet? (Dawk)

A dragon. (Hype)

And you're still alive? (Dawk)

Hype ignored her brother and peered into the space that the doorway led to. It wasn't very impressive—just a small and dirty passage that led to another door. She walked down the passage, opened the door, and peered in. There were several more long passages, each lined with lit torches. Still, she couldn't see much.

She chose one path and walked to the end, only to find three more paths.

Didn't Rome have a maze? NeuroNet doesn't reference a maze, but I'm almost sure there was a PlayMod about it. (Hype)

You're thinking of Greece. (Fizzbin)

But I'm in Rome and I think I'm in a maze. (Hype)

If the OpBot were with you, I could use it to clarify your position. (Fizzbin)

I'll just choose another corridor and move on. (Hype)

The hallway she chose ended in another door. She kept going. Every possible choice led to a door that inevitably led to more possible choices and more doors. Choices and doors, over and over.

Finally, one door was different. She clasped the handle and pulled slowly, sure she'd just see more hallways and more doors.

But instead, she saw a huge room overloaded with machinery and machine parts piled high. There were men huddled all around, clunking and clanking while they worked on their contraptions, making such a racket that Hype felt sure you would be able to hear it aboveground very easily. Soldiers and servants were hurriedly crisscrossing the area. The whole scene was confusing.

"Antevorta requested refreshment," came a woman's voice.

A carafe was shoved at Hype and she grabbed

it. She didn't know what was happening, but she didn't want to let the frosted glass carafe fall and break, drawing attention to herself. She looked up. Standing in front of her was a harsh-looking woman with squinty, mean eyes and unwashed hair.

"Move!" the woman snapped. "Don't get me in trouble with Antevorta because you poke along!"

Hype nodded quickly and dashed into the crowd before her. She had no idea who Antevorta was or where to find her. Quick access of the general level of NeuroPedia yielded nothing immediate, and she was finding it hard to negotiate the crowd and also quickly research Antevorta on NeuroPedia at the same time.

Could you please find out about someone named Antevorta, Fizzbin? And also underground chambers in Rome? (Hype)

I'm already searching deeper in the history banks for information about Antevorta, but general level cross-referencing has only brought up the Hypogeum, a huge network of passages and chambers underneath the Colosseum. That seems unlikely, however, since the Colosseum will not be completed until 80 AD and the

Hypogeum was not unveiled until ten years after that. (Fizzbin)

It couldn't be that anyhow. The cave entrance is way outside of Rome. Keep looking. And Dawk? Where are you? (Hype)

Eating olives with Pliny outside the cave. Well, he's eating and I'm forcing them into my face. And he's insisting we wait for you. (Dawk)

I don't know how to get you out of that one. Sorry. (Hype)

Hype kept walking, shielding the carafe close to avoid a mishap that would call attention to herself. But she still didn't know where she was meant to be taking it.

"I'll report back to Antevorta myself," she heard someone say.

It was one of the old gladiator guys from the dragon cave. He nodded to his comrade and they went in opposite directions. Hype followed the one going to see Antevorta. It seemed like a good start to figuring out what was going on down there.

The old gladiator trod through the crowd until he reached another passage, which he entered.

Hype silently padded a bit behind him. She didn't want to seem like she was following him.

I have some information about Antevorta. It would seem she was one of the lesser Roman gods, specifically the goddess of the future. (Fizzbin)

Do you think it's the same Antevorta? (Hype)

That is harder to answer. Antevorta is traditionally known for helping women in childbirth and for bickering with her sister, Postverta. They are not the sort of A-list gods that find themselves at the center of popular PlayMods, like Mercury or Jupiter. (Fizzbin)

No, I mean, do you think she's real? (Hype)

All I think is that you have heard of someone with that name, and the only person I can find with that name is a minor Roman goddess. We'll find out more when you make your delivery. (Fizzbin)

A gladiator guy approached an open chamber off the side of the torch-lined corridor. Hype remained what she thought was a safe distance away as she watched him enter, and then sped up to the entrance and stood to one side in order to concentrate on the voices in the room.

" . . . the creature was exactly as you described,

and was duly resuscitated," she heard the gladiator say. "Although any explanation for the dragon's collapse was not obvious in the cave."

"That is unimportant," came a female voice. "If you were younger, I might well say you had a future as a physician for dragons."

"Your luminosity is too kind."

"Not at all," the woman said. "You are dismissed with sincere thanks, Fulgentius."

Hype heard the gladiator's footsteps coming near her. As he turned the corner at the chamber entrance, he stopped and glanced at her. "She will have her refreshment now, girl," he said and moved on.

Hype nodded and moved slowly to the doorway and into the room, which seemed like a human-made cave. It was lit by a number of clay oil lamps placed in a makeshift mantle that had been carved in the stone wall. Inside were several women, several guards, and a few old men, all sitting around and staring at scrolls. At the farthest end of the room sat a woman with raven black hair, a white garment, and an unnerving glow.

Literally. It seemed to Hype that the woman's skin actually glistened.

This had to be Antevorta.

Everyone else in the room was sitting on benches, but Antevorta was sitting on an unusual chair that had ornate, curved legs and appeared to be made out of ivory. The chair had an upper loop that nestled her and allowed her to recline forward. It was very odd, but it made her look quite important.

"Refreshment!" Antevorta said, beaming. "Please, girl, come closer! I'm parched."

Hype slowly walked toward Antevorta, who held out a goblet. Hype filled the goblet. Antevorta sipped it in an appreciative way, and smiled. "I have not seen you here before," the woman said. "Are you a new girl?"

"Yes, your luminosity," Hype said quietly.

"Well, you are far more pleasant than some they've had tripping about. Are you from Rome, or further lands?"

"Rome, your luminosity."

"Ah. Well I am from Mount Olympus. I prefer the climate here in Rome."

"Underground, you mean?" Hype asked.

"Ah, a pouring girl with a quick mind! You'll soon move beyond carafes." Antevorta motioned to one of the old men, who jumped up and skipped over to her. "Balbinus, I would like this girl as my attendant," she said. "Please send the other one to the kitchens. She spilled so often. I would like her to wield the mop there."

"Y-yes, your radiance!" the man said. He grabbed the arm of a girl nearby and dragged her out of the room.

"And you, new girl, what is your name?" Antevorta asked.

"Hypatia, your radiance."

Antevorta smiled. "What a beautiful name," she said.

Antevorta is at least acting like a real goddess, and her presence is luminescent or irradiated or something. (Hype)

Perhaps she's a mutant. (Fizzbin)

She's asked me to be her attendant. Well, asked isn't the right word. (Hype)

There are several options to—(Fizzbin)

Then, suddenly, Fizzbin was gone.

The Link was gone.

Hype tried to tap into any sort of streaming, to access Dawk, anything. It was all gone. She had lost the Link before, when they were in Prague—but at least Dawk had been with her that time. Now she was in 75 AD without a safety net.

"Valeriana!" Antevorta snapped her fingers and a very short girl came forward.

"Please show Hypatia to the servants' quarters and her new bed," Antevorta said. "This is a new life for her," she added, looking carefully at Hype, "and since she is cut off from whatever she has held dear, I want her to know the comfort and safety provided that might move her to hold me dear instead."

Valeriana took Hype by the elbow, nodded and smiled, pulling her away from Antevorta. If Hype didn't know any better, she'd swear that Antevorta knew about the Link and knew Hype had been disconnected from it. When Hype turned her head, Antevorta's narrowed eyes were watching her leave, like a predator looking at lunch.

Maybe Hype did know better, after all.

CHAPTER

9

Outside the cave, Dawk was bored by Pliny, who had been going on about his knowledge of caves. He knew a lot about things like stalactites and stalagmites, but Dawk was too worried about his sister to listen to Pliny talking about minerals.

Fizzbin. You found her yet? (Dawk)

I don't know what knocked her off-Link and I'm working to reestablish her access. In the meantime, I have sent the OpBot back into the cave in order to assess the situation and hopefully find your sister. It can then bring her back. (Fizzbin)

If we don't get her back out here by nighttime, what are we going to tell Mom and Dad? (Dawk)

I believe that falls into your field of expertise, not mine. (Fizzbin)

"We can probably go back now!" Dawk said, and pushed back the bowl of olives.

"What I don't understand is how you know we can go back," Pliny explained.

Dawk began walking back to Rome. "Just come with me and I'll explain it."

They walked away from the cave, but Dawk didn't say a word. He was too busy concentrating on the Link in hopes that somehow Hype would appear.

"Silence will not excuse you from my curiosity," Pliny said. "What goes on in your brain that causes you to ignore me?"

"I wasn't ignoring you. I was concentrating on something else," said Dawk.

"Fearing for your sister," Pliny said, nodding.

"You're a man of science," Dawk said slowly, trying to figure out just what to say. "What would you say if I told you that Hype and I have a special link? I can hear her with that link and I was listening for her."

What are you doing, Dawk? (Fizzbin)

I need him to trust me if this is going to go smoothly. Besides, he's a genius. He'd probably figure it out sooner or later. (Dawk)

"Are you saying you hear things?" Pliny asked. "A buzzing, perhaps?"

Dawk nodded. "Sort of," he said.

Pliny laughed. "Nothing a few earthworms boiled in goose grease won't fix right up. When we return to my chambers, I will apply the remedy to your ears."

"I don't hear her in my ears," Dawk said, trying to explain. "It's more like . . . it's like I hear her in my brain."

"The brain is the seat of the mind's government. And I take it your sister has a special ability to stand before it at any moment?"

"Something like that," Dawk muttered.

"I've heard of such things among seers, priestesses, and the like, and though I thought it might have some relation to the tides as well, I see no evidence," said Pliny. "A seer sees regardless of where the ocean falls. I believe you."

The man is not a genius. He is obsessed with tides. It's as if a tide crashed into his brain and gave him ridiculous notions. (Fizzbin)

Dawk chuckled to himself and decided to let the Link stream freely, giving PlayModCulture a chance to drown out Fizzbin on the walk back to Rome.

◦◎ ❖ ◎◦

It was nearly dusk by the time they got back to Rome. Pliny went home, and Dawk walked back to his family's house.

He decided to turn down the Link input he was receiving so that Fizzbin could get through more easily. If something did happen to Hype, he wanted to know about it. And if something didn't happen to Hype, he wanted to figure out what he could do about it.

Hype was still off-Link.

Any updates? (Dawk)

The OpBot arrived at the cave, found the dragon, and

promptly revealed its heat shielding to be inadequate. I'm afraid we have to wait on reconnaissance. (Fizzbin)

What does that mean? The OpBot caught fire? (Dawk)

The OpBot traveled too close to a gust of the dragon's breath and was trapped by a burst of fire. It received enough surface damage that its internal circuits switched all concerns to maintenance and it promptly fizzled out. I've had it transferred back to the twenty-fifth century and requested a replacement. We need to be more careful with the creature in the cave. (Fizzbin)

So we're going to have to cover for Hype until the unit is replaced and can get back down there? (Dawk)

Exactly. And if they fail to provide us with a model that boasts a higher-grade shielding, I'm afraid we won't be able to collect the proper data about the dragon. (Fizzbin)

Data on the dragon comes second to Hype. We need to find her and get her back before Mom and Dad find out. Or worse, the Chancellor. (Dawk)

You just leave everything to me. (Fizzbin)

Dawk wasn't so sure he should. The last time he'd left everything to Fizzbin, he and his sister had found themselves darting through Prague, jumping between centuries, being chased by alchemist thugs, and having no idea where they would end up. Fizzbin's track record wasn't exactly stellar.

Finally home, Dawk found supper was already waiting, and Mom and Dad hadn't bothered to wait. They were sitting down, stuffing bread and meat into their faces as fast as they could.

"I never thought this could be so exhausting," Dad told Dawk as he took his place at the table. "It's a constant battle with Vespasian, who doesn't want to address shoes in any way whatsoever."

"And we can't complain about the assignment," Mom said. "Just the fact that the Emperor avoids the slightest mention of shoes means that the information about shoes and his involvement with the shoes of this era is so much more precious and worth uncovering. The very difficulty of this assignment is an argument for being forced to stick with it!"

"Which is incredibly frustrating," Dad said, "because the man will not talk about shoes. He will talk about robes and staffs and grooming and chairs and plenty of other things, but shoes do not figure into his conversations."

They shoveled down some more dinner before Mom spoke up again. "Grab some food before we take it all. And where is your sister?"

"Doing field study for Pliny," Dawk said. "Nocturnal creatures. His eyesight isn't so good in the dark, so Hype's helping him out. Plus she's got the OpBot, so she can slip in a little extra to help the old guy out."

"Well, she could have accessed us through the Link and told us herself," Dad said. "When will she be back?"

"She won't be, at least not tonight. She's camping."

"Camping?" Dad repeated. "Aren't there lions or bull monsters or something on the loose in the countryside here?"

I have arranged for Hype's visual cortex shell to act as a deterrent in case of an encounter with a predator. There are several predetermined settings for specific situations involving deadly animals and I have taken the precaution of enacting those for her. (Fizzbin)

"I've never heard of this!" marveled Dad. "Is this new technology?"

It's something they are rolling out to temporal researchers on an as-needed basis. (Fizzbin)

Dawk was quite impressed by Fizzbin's mistruth programming, but it also made him a little wary. If every IntelliBoard in the banks of the Alvarium had top-quality mistruth programming as a standard feature, who knows what they could do?

It made Dawk pretty nervous, and he did have to wonder if Fizzbin was being honest about Hype. Fizzbin made it all seem solvable, but Dawk wondered if he should be a lot more worried than he already was.

CHAPTER 10

Hype sat quietly on the hard cot and stared at all the others like it in the servants' quarters. Valeriana had introduced her to the space with a mix of nervousness and fear. It seemed to Hype that Valeriana didn't want to appear unhappy with her lot in life. The other girl was afraid that Antevorta would react like the typical Roman goddess who didn't like how humans were behaving.

Roman goddess? Sure. She didn't know what else to think Antevorta was, no clue at all, anymore than she knew how to explain the dragon. It was a real dragon she saw, she felt sure of that because she had seen it up close with her own two eyes. She just didn't completely understand what it was doing down here, since all history banks claim that dragons were only imaginary creatures.

"She wants to see you," someone said. It was Valeriana. "In her chambers. She wants to make sure you know how to navigate your new position."

"Shouldn't you be checking me for all that?" Hype asked.

Valeriana shrugged. "She's taken a personal interest in you. Perhaps you'll be important in times to come. She would be the one to know."

Hype didn't know what else to do, so she followed Valeriana through the corridors and to Antevorta's chambers. There were guards in front, but the two girls were allowed in right away.

Antevorta was sitting on a giant cushion, reading some scrolls. She was still all aglow. She looked up calmly as the girls entered. "Thank you, Valeriana," she said. "Back to your duties."

Valeriana bowed quickly and left the room. Hype stood there, not sure what to expect.

"Hypatia, I wanted to personally help settle you into your new surroundings," Antevorta said. "This is, after all, where you are going to spend the rest of your days, so I'd prefer you to become comfortable as soon as possible. That way your remaining time can be orderly and peaceful. There's no need for you to go through an uncertain period of settling, do you think?"

"You are the goddess of the future," Hype murmured, nodding. "You are the seer from on high, your luminosity, it's you who knows best what I need."

Not bad, Hype thought. *Not bad at all.*

"Your primary duty will be pouring," Antevorta went on. "From what I have seen, you are fairly expert at that. A master pourer!"

There seemed to be a mocking tone in Antevorta's voice, but why was she making fun of Hype? For being an ordinary mortal? For being a servant? This was a horrible time for Hype's Link access to be missing. Fizzbin would certainly have something to say in order to help.

"Thank you, your luminosity. With pourers on

Mount Olympus as my comparison, that is surely a high honor."

"Mount Olympus must seem so far away to one such as you," Antevorta said. "Even the servants there are removed from the life of an ordinary girl, Roman or not."

"To be a servant on Mount Olympus would be one of my greatest goals," Hype said.

"You may sit," Antevorta said, and tapped down on the cushion. "There's enough room for a mortal servant, but please pour me a refreshment before resting."

Hype did as she was instructed, handing Antevorta a goblet and then sitting down.

"Do you want to hear all about Olympus?" Antevorta said.

Yes, thought Hype, *but only so I can compare it to what NeuroPedia says about it in order to figure out who exactly you are.* She'd have to attempt to cache Antevorta's stories in her neural bypass chip and then upload them to Fizzbin when she got Link access again.

If she got Link access again.

What if Antevorta was right? What if Hype was going to spend the rest of her life as a servant girl pouring refreshments to mysterious goddesses in underground complexes in the ancient Roman Empire?

Hype gently shook her head. She couldn't think about that possibility.

"Of course you do," Antevorta said. "What mortal girl does not want to hear about the wonders of a world she could never live in, where everything is perfect? Almost all—well, some—of the male gods like to belch a bit too often for my taste, and being goddess of the future, I can see that that won't end anytime soon. They'll just keep burping until the end of the world. Other than that, Mount Olympus is everything that you can never have."

"How do you pass your time on Mount Olympus, your luminosity?"

Antevorta sighed. "We like our ambrosia and nectar, and sometimes mushrooms of a certain variety. We lie around and strum on our lyres. I will admit, I am a lesser goddess. I accept my lot in existence; I am not ashamed. All the big stuff, the praise and priestesses and festivals, are for the likes of Venus and Vesta and, of course, Minerva, that know-it-all. Not that I'm jealous—Minerva might be the goddess of wisdom, but she can't tell you what's coming. Only I can do that."

"If perfection reigns, then why don't you stay there and enjoy the ambrosia, your luminosity?" Hype asked. "Why stain yourself with the dirt of humanity?"

"Ambrosia and nectar is all very nice, but it's terribly boring there," Antevorta admitted. "It's so boring that all we gods and goddesses ever do is bicker and play tricks on each other, all of which gets doubly boring after a while. And so I came down and made this city under the dirt. On the earth above this very room, there will one day be an altar used for sacrifices to Jupiter and Pluto, even Diana. I told you, girl, I know very well what's coming. Down here, I will rule. And soon enough, I will have more than enough persuasion on the surface of Rome."

"What do you call this divine hole that you've built?" asked Hype.

Before Antevorta could answer, Valeriana entered. "Your visitor has arrived, your luminosity," she said.

"Show him in," the goddess replied. "You may go now, Hypatia. I will see you tomorrow to pour for me."

Hype nodded and began to walk out when another figure entered. A man. It was Domitian, Titus's brother and the Emperor's son, who Hype had met earlier in Pliny's quarters. Hype tried to hide her surprise. Domitian seemed unlikable, but she hadn't guessed he had anything to do with Antevorta.

She turned her face down as if she were shy, which was probably appropriate behavior for a servant. Domitian didn't seem to notice her anyhow. He breezed right past her and directly toward the radiant goddess who awaited him.

CHAPTER

11

Dawk was asleep when he heard a voice calmly repeating his name. Was it a dream? He opened his eyes, but couldn't see anything in his room because it was so dark. He was groggy enough that it took him a moment to realize it was Fizzbin waking him up through the Link.

Yeah? (Dawk)

Benton sent back a new OpBot to the last coordinates reported by the previous one. I've shut off its autonomy programming and have it currently in position for visuals and audio, if you are awake. (Fizzbin)

Thanks to you, yes, I am. (Dawk)

The OpBot's visuals and audio began streaming through Dawk's mind via the NeuroNet. It was in the cave that they had been in earlier, and had come upon a lump of scaly flesh that had to be the dragon. The huge beast was asleep. The OpBot lingered slowly while it was close to the dragon so it could run a scan and feed the data back to Fizzbin for processing before skittering away deeper into the underground complex.

Scans indicate that the dragon is a biological creature, made of natural tissue—but also with all the hallmarks of synthetic tissue. (Fizzbin)

What does that mean? (Dawk)

The DNA is odd. (Fizzbin)

What does that mean? (Dawk)

It should reflect a history of this dragon's species or family, but there's nothing in it other than the fact of this dragon being this dragon. (Fizzbin)

I don't get it. (Dawk)

This animal has had no changes in its biology, no evolutionary history. It's almost as if it was created as is. Also, some coding is blank and that seems to correspond with missing parts of the dragon, like tonsils and tear ducts, things that you might find on a real animal. And no ear muscles, which all animals have. Very curious. (Fizzbin)

What are ear muscles for? (Dawk)

Animals can't move their ears without those. I don't know why a dragon wouldn't need to move its ears. (Fizzbin)

The OpBot continued floating on, following scans that indicated living, breathing humans. It wound through the passages, under doorways, and around feet.

Are you mapping the area while the OpBot buzzes through? (Dawk)

Of course. And if you're feeling daring, you might need that data. It will also make a fine addition to the Rome banks in NeuroPedia. (Fizzbin)

Good for future PlayMods, too. (Dawk)

The OpBot came out of the maze-like passageways and into a larger room. It was filled with huge metal structures.

What is all that junk? (Dawk)

A quick cross-reference reveals that this is not junk at

all, but the future of the Hypogeum. These will all be used in an intricate system of elevators, pulleys, and such that will move items around for future shows. There is also a hydraulic system linked to an aqueduct, and the OpBot registers some more sophisticated machinery that I have not yet been able to identify. (Fizzbin)

Hype had confused the place with a maze of some sort, and Dawk could see why. The underground structure seemed like it was designed to confuse on purpose. The OpBot went through several more corridors before it began to register what looked like private quarters—opulent ones, at that.

"I just don't understand how you are able to guarantee that I will defeat the dragon," came a male voice. The OpBot followed it.

Did you hear that? (Dawk)

"You are questioning my prowess, Domitian?" a woman's voice replied. "You think a child of Olympus cannot control the whims of a dumb beast such as a dragon?"

The OpBot is following the voice waves currently and will try to get closer. (Fizzbin)

"I do not think dragons are dumb beasts," the man said, "but if anything or anyone in creation could hold sway over one, it would certainly be your luminosity."

"And your victory in saving Rome from such a hellion will be followed by the appearance of this child of Olympus, who will command the hero be handed control."

"With your luminosity as his Caesaris, yes."

I'm running a face scan, and it is confirming—(Fizzbin)

Domitian. That's Domitian. He's a big jerk. What about the lady? (Dawk)

Face scan is useless on her, but I'm sure you can take a valid guess yourself. (Fizzbin)

Antevorta. (Dawk)

"All plans have been fully completed to my satisfaction," Antevorta said. "The mechanisms are nearly ready, and will be perfect for the Circus of Antevorta, certain to become an amusement and fear factory for good Romans. They will be quite aware that I know everyone's fate, and when called to battle an errant bear or lion in the Colosseum, they will learn that my pronouncement is something to be feared."

"And once the people understand who dictates their fate, that will allow us to prepare our forces to move toward Mount Olympus itself and take it!" Domitian said. "All of Rome is too small for the two of us."

This is all becoming more clear. The goddess and the Emperor's son are planning on controlling citizens through fear and tricking them into defeating the Roman gods. (Fizzbin)

Do you think they can do that? (Dawk)

I've run all other possible outcomes for analysis. Only a few of them result in taking Rome. None of them result in conquering Mount Olympus, since that location does not really exist. (Fizzbin)

Dawk watched the scenery whiz by as the OpBot zoomed back to the general area.

I'm having the OpBot scan for Hype's neural bypass anywhere on the premises. (Fizzbin)

Once the OpBot got the signal, it moved along quickly and made its way into a large room and hovered down on a bed, just above Hype.

She was fast asleep.

So, what, she's a captive down there and still getting a better sleep than I am? (Dawk)

I've run some diagnostics. (Fizzbin)

And? (Dawk)

There is nothing wrong with Hype's bypass and the NeuroNet temporal pathway is strong. I am beaming data directly to her bypass's cache that she will be able to access later on. (Fizzbin)

Fizzbin directed the OpBot back to the large room with all the machinery. It moved in closely around the contraptions and continued upward to show the wooden ceiling.

Dawk spotted levers that went to pulleys and connected to valves that turned gears that would move belts. These were all connected in a number of ways to small sections that looked like they were equipped with sliders and lifts and still more gears and pulleys.

It all looked very complicated.

The OpBot hovered near one of the valves. It set forth a slight magnetic beam that moved it counterclockwise.

Note the slight movement in the ceiling, specifically a panel that has moved aside ever so slightly. The OpBot has registered a draft coming through that. (Fizzbin)

What does that mean? Surface? (Dawk)

Shall we see? (Fizzbin)

The OpBot hovered higher until it finally slipped through the small opening. There was a brief moment where Dawk could see the kind of materials that could be expected—wood and concrete, specifically—but then . . . nothing. Total darkness.

Is it stuck? (Dawk)

It's still moving upward. (Fizzbin)

It was a few moments later when the OpBot's surroundings became a little more visible, though still vague due to darkness. It began to soar higher— at least it was no longer constrained in a tiny space—and kept going until it was obviously high enough in the sky to reveal a beautiful view of the center of Rome in the twilight.

The OpBot's trajectory has made the situation very clear. (Fizzbin)

Did it just go straight up? (Dawk)

Yes. It seems the underground where Hype and the dragon and the mysterious goddess and Domitian are all gathered is located directly beneath the Colosseum. It's right in the middle of Rome. (Fizzbin)

CHAPTER

12

Dawk didn't get much sleep the rest of the night, partly from worry about Hype and partly from pure excitement. It was strange to know that the next day might hold some adventure involving the secret underground lair of a Roman goddess—and maybe even the dragon again.

When he got out of bed, he grabbed a hunk of bread. Then he dashed out. He was anxious to get going, and he was hoping to get over to Pliny's before Mom and Dad woke up. They were grumpy these days, since their job was just one frustrating day after another of attempting to get Emperor Vespasian to say something—anything—on the subject of shoes.

Dawk was headed to Pliny's with the OpBot in tow. He knew what he had to explain to Pliny, but he hadn't quite figured how to say it.

The dragon was just the tip of the iceberg. Would Pliny be able to accept that it was being kept as a pet and used for a plot against the Emperor and his son by his other son? That it was being kept underneath the city of Rome?

Emperor Vespasian was Pliny's boss, and Titus his patron, so he might be immediately worried and protective.

But Pliny would certainly want an actual peek at the real, live, actual dragon being held underground. Dawk was sure of that.

How to do it without being scorched to death was a whole other question.

⊙⊚ ❖ ⊚⊙

When Dawk arrived, Pliny was with Titus and

Domitian. Titus greeted Dawk while Domitian just stared at them.

"I am informing Titus of additional facts in our studies about the dragon," Pliny said, smiling.

"Which further facts do you mean?" Dawk asked cautiously.

"The attack on the forest and the further flight," Pliny said. "What more have we to report?"

"I would say that's more than enough, Pliny," Titus replied. "Not only is your work advancing the cause of the natural sciences, it's providing security for Rome. Thanks to you we can be assured that any rumors we hear are not just rumors, and we can be at the ready."

"My brother seems keen to kill a dragon," said Domitian, "though less keen to reveal how."

"You stab it in each of its hearts," Titus said with a laugh. "How many hearts does a dragon have, Pliny?"

"That's something I hope to find out once you dispatch the creature," Pliny told him. "Which creates a certain conflict for you, I understand, since you need that information up front."

"You'll just have to stab first and ask questions later," said Dawk, which sent the three men into hysterics.

"Well! The boy is not quite the dolt he seemed," said Domitian.

Is there something the OpBot can do to hurt that guy? (Dawk)

The OpBot is not designated for cruel usage or any sort of harm, Dawk. I am truly sorry. (Fizzbin)

Just fusing his mouth closed would be good enough for me. (Dawk)

That does officially count as a medical procedure—which the OpBot is permitted for—but it might not be the best idea. (Fizzbin)

Seems like a good idea to me. (Dawk)

Your suggestion will be taken under consideration. (Fizzbin)

All I want is to be taken seriously. (Dawk)

"We'll leave you to your dragon hunting," Titus said and patted Pliny on the back. "Just don't let this tangent distract you from other disciplines within the natural sciences. And do get back to me about the number of hearts."

You will not be surprised to find that even with his short reign, Titus was immensely more beloved an Emperor than Domitian was. (Fizzbin)

As Titus and Domitian left, Pliny hustled to Dawk's side.

"And have you news from your sister through your astounding mind link?" asked Pliny.

"I know exactly where she is," Dawk said, "and you're not going to believe it. I just have one question—do you think you can use your rank to get us into the Colosseum site?"

CHAPTER 13

Pliny and Dawk walked along the perimeter of the Colosseum until they hit an official checkpoint that would lead them inside the construction.

"I am in charge of the Vigiles, as you should know, though you can check that with Vespasian himself," Pliny told the guard on duty. "Even better—get permission from Titus to allow us in."

"Sir?" the guard asked.

"He is the sponsor of my encyclopedias, and he is fanatical about the natural sciences. He wants me to find a specimen of the Amphitheater mouse—

mus amphitheatrum—in hopes of studying it and preventing it from doing its usual destruction."

"Amphitheater mouse?" the guard repeated.

"Have you never heard of these vicious pests?" Pliny asked. "If allowed to breed, they can take down an Amphitheater within a day of building it, so powerful are their teeth. Surely you don't want that to happen to this structure?"

"Of course not!" the guard said, shocked.

"Then let us in, man, let us in, and leave us to our job! If it goes too far it will be as head of the Vigiles that you see me next, and I will not be smiling!"

The guard let them pass. Dawk and Pliny wandered in, moving toward the open-air stage in the center. Dawk was amazed at how near completion the place seemed. There couldn't be much left to do before they started putting on their infamously bloody shows. Those shows were the inspiration for many PlayMods that a certain type in PlayModCulture couldn't get enough of.

"Do you have any idea how to access the level in which Hypatia is being held?" asked Pliny.

I have a map prepared for you, Dawk. If you will grant access, please. (Fizzbin)

Dawk felt the map directed at him and approved it. The real world of the Colosseum melted away and the CartoMod version took its place. CartoMods were just like any other mod, without the complete interactivity. It was really just a map that beamed into your brain. Instead of seeing the space you were actually in, you saw the CartoMod, which was an exact replica of wherever you were, plus directional help.

"Or are you just wandering as blind as I?" Pliny asked.

Dawk had forgotten that Pliny was there. "No, no, I think I've got it," Dawk said, noting the blue star ahead of him that was leading the way.

"Ah, you are communicating with her now!" Pliny said. "Please inform her that I admire her bravery and look forward to discussing dragon anatomy with her."

"Consider it done." Dawk didn't want to explain that Hype couldn't access the Link.

Dawk had been in thousands of PlayMods and

educational mods in his life, but never one that took place on top of reality.

It was hard for him to walk. If Fizzbin had done the job thoroughly, there would be no opportunity for Dawk to bump into anything at all, but his brain wasn't used to this dynamic.

Physically, it felt like walking through darkness, since he was so concerned with encountering an object not on the CartoMod that his arms were out and flailing around, and his footsteps careful. He looked like a puppet with strings.

You're looking for a trap door. (Fizzbin)

What's a trap door? (Dawk)

You'll only really know for sure once you find it. (Fizzbin)

Thanks for the help. (Dawk)

Dawk stumbled along while Pliny chattered on about the design. Dawk wanted to let the Link stream through his brain to drown out Pliny's architectural nitpicking, but he knew Fizzbin would never let that pass. And that annoyed him enough to—

Dawk didn't have a chance to finish that thought.

Suddenly, the floor disappeared from under him and he found himself tumbling downward. The CartoMod reflected the confusion that must be going on outside his brain, even up to the point he found himself doing a final somersault and landing flat on his back.

That was a trap door. (Fizzbin)

CHAPTER

14

Waking up off-Link was a very strange experience for Hype. It would definitely take some getting used to. When she woke up in the twenty-fifth century—which wasn't so often anymore—Mom would immediately stream a "coffee ready in the NutroFabricator" wake-up message. If they were on a temporal job, she would at least get NeuroHugs.

Here, nothing. Nothing, that is, but a bunch of other servant girls hustling around at the sound of a loud bell, getting themselves ready for a day of attending the goddess of the future as she prepared to enact her wacky plan, which required lots and lots of help feeding herself and fluffing up her pillows.

Hype gulped down the servants' breakfast, a sort of grain-based porridge. It would have been good with something sweet added to it, but was barely swallowable as it was. She couldn't even imagine how to coax disgusting slop like that out of a NutroFabricator. In the twenty-fifth century, there was no such thing as a yucky meal.

As she trudged on toward her chore—her only real chore, refilling the decanter and going to serve whatever was in it to Antevorta and her guests—she wondered if she would ever taste anything out of a NutroFabricator again.

Would the Cosmos Institute be able to find her and steal her away? Or could her parents?

Maybe she would have to escape. She wasn't sure how she could do that without Link access, but then she reminded herself that she was a time traveler. Time travelers, in general, were not timid or dull.

Surely she could figure out some way to escape. After all, she knew some secret passages.

She clutched the carafe tightly as she approached Antevorta's chamber.

"Finally! I am parched!" screamed Antevorta when Hype entered the room. "I see you still need some lessons in being prompt, Hypatia."

Antevorta gestured for her. Hype couldn't understand what the point of being a goddess was if you got thirsty. She poured water into Antevorta's goblet, which the goddess was holding out to her impatiently.

"What should we do about your tardiness?" Antevorta asked. "Shall I run you on drills? Have you march back to your quarters and then march here again, onward and onward, until you learn punctuality worthy of the goddess of the future?"

That was another thing that bothered Hype. The woman could supposedly see everything that was to happen.

Why was it she couldn't see what time Hype would show up? Did even the all-knowing have to pick and choose what they pay attention to?

"Truly, I think that must be what's done," Antevorta said. "Hypatia, go back and do it all again.

I expect you to be here following a faster pace than before. You really must get this right if you are going to serve."

Hype smiled, bowed, and went back through the entrance. Once out of the sight of Antevorta, she began dashing through busy crowds of people. Who were they, anyhow? They always seemed to be going to and fro and never stopping anywhere to do anything at all.

She turned a sharp corner that led to two hallways. Should she start back at her quarters and then get the carafe refilled? Or should she take care of the refill first? Too confusing for something so unimportant. She decided to head to the kitchens to get the carafe filled, then to the servant quarters, so she headed to the left fork.

"You there, water girl, some refreshment is needed here!"

The voice came from the side, a shadowy figure nestled so perfectly next to a column that she could barely make out anything about the person. He was older. Fulgentius? She didn't know it was her duty to refill the cups of soldiers and guards, but she thought it best not to take anything for granted around there, and obediently marched over to him.

As she got closer, she saw that it was Pliny.

"Hello, Hypatia."

Then she noticed a figure off the side, carefully remaining behind the column. It was Dawk.

"We're here to rescue you," he said, smiling.

"Surely she knew that," Pliny said.

"What?" asked Hype.

"Surely your brother informed you of the plan through your special ways and that is why you came here looking for us."

"Exactly," Dawk said. "That's exactly what I did. Right, Hype? You came here knowing that we were here waiting for you."

"Oh, yeah," Hype said. "Of course."

"It's a marvel to me that either of you bother to talk to each other," Pliny said. "Such a waste of your mouths."

Dawk shrugged his shoulders and looked at Hype, his eyebrows high and smile dumb, and then grabbed her and dragged her behind the column.

"We're going to have to do this in an orderly

way, and we're going to have to use our mouths so Pliny can take in all the information," Dawk muttered. "You tell us what you know and I'll tell you what we know, and somewhere in between, I bet we can figure out what to do."

Hype began with her part—Antevorta was a goddess from Mount Olympus who, bored, had come down to create her own hangout space in Rome and meet up with Domitian. It all sounded ridiculous, really.

"Then I can tell you where this is all going," Dawk said. "Antevorta is in control of the dragon and is plotting with Domitian to fabricate a battle that he will win so he can take control of Rome. Once that's done, Antevorta wants to use the Roman legions to march on Mount Olympus. Oh, and we're in the Hypogeum, which, it turns out, was built at least a decade before it was supposed to be built and that's part of the plan to control the Romans through fear and violence."

"Surely, Hype told you this?" asked Pliny.

"One of the crazy parts of our powers is that we forget what we tell each other," Dawk said.

"Right after we transmit it, it's gone. So we have to remind each other and we have to do it by mouth, because if we do it by mind waves, it's like volleying information back and forth that keeps being forgotten by the one sending it. Right, Hype?"

Hype rolled her eyes. "So what's our top priority?" she asked. "Stop Domitian? Stop the dragon? Stop Antevorta? Stop whoever built the Hypogeum? Stop whatever's blocking my NeuroNet access?"

Dawk let out a nervous chuckle and shook his head. "Fizzbin said to tell you, 'All of the above,'" he said.

CHAPTER

15

Ask her if she has any more information on Antevorta being a goddess. (Fizzbin)

"Do you know anything more about Antevorta being a goddess or whatever?" Dawk asked.

"Why do you want to know?" Hype asked.

"I don't want to know. *He* wants to know," Dawk said, gesturing to Pliny.

Hype looked at Pliny. "Why do you want to know?"

"Why do I want to know what?" Pliny asked, frowning.

"Why do you want to know about Antevorta?" Dawk asked slowly, as if Pliny were a toddler.

"Antevorta?" Pliny chuckled. "Now there is a divine name one doesn't hear too often, especially if one is of the male variety. She is concerned with the future, but also childbirth. I don't get involved with that nonsense except for research purposes."

"Is she a powerful goddess?" Hype asked.

"Not particularly," Pliny said, shrugging. "One half of the Carmentae, with her sister, Postverta. The stories have it that they were both the nymph Carmenta, different aspects of her, but over time, they manifested themselves separately. As the goddess of the future, Antevorta is certainly more powerful than her sister, who presides over the past. Hindsight is a horrible power to have, but we all have it, don't we?"

"I think I'd rather be facing off against her sister," Dawk said. "At least she'd have no idea what we were going to do next."

"Just like us," added Hype.

After making a risk analysis and calculating probabilities of paradox, from lowest to highest, I would suggest tackling the dragon first, both figuratively and literally, since it stands at the center of Antevorta's plan and has already been put into motion. Historically speaking, there are sightings of dragons, so nothing has been tampered with in any meaningful way thus far. And the curious nature of its biology is no doubt irrelevant to the issue. The harder part will be dealing with the Hypogeum, particularly whatever technology exists down here that shouldn't, and Antevorta herself, who I would wager is not a goddess at all, but a fellow time traveler. (Fizzbin)

"Fizzbin says to deal with the dragon first," Dawk said. "And that technology is here that shouldn't be."

Actually, I said much more than that, but I see your point. (Fizzbin)

"This is the second time we've found temporal tampering in the past," Hype said, "but this one goes way beyond the discarded hardware in Prague. This is like a . . . a plot."

"But a really dumb one," Dawk said. "I mean, who cares if someone became the Roman Emperor before history says he did? Who cares if some underground lair was built before history claims it was? Who cares if one dragon really does exist after all? What does this matter in the big scheme of things?"

"Well, Domitian certainly wouldn't allow me to remain the upcoming prefect of the Royal Navy were he to become Emperor now," Pliny said. "His father has that post scheduled for me following finishing touches on my encyclopedia."

"That's not a major difference," Hype said.

"It is for me," Pliny said. "He would retire me, which means I would spend the rest of my life in Rome. That would be tiresome. So much to see and do in the world."

A quick scan of Pliny's bio-banks in NeuroPedia tells me that could change history in a major, though unpredictable, way. It is unfortunately Pliny's fate to die during the eruption of Vesuvius in Pompeii, which he goes to visit only because Vespasian has made him prefect of the Navy. Pliny's suggestion is that Domitian could cause a disruption in history out of spite. (Fizzbin)

So you're saying that this comes down to a decision between Pliny living and dying? We have to save his life. That's the right thing to do. (Dawk)

It would be the right thing to do if we were of this time, but to us, Pliny has already died. That happened in history. I exist in the twenty-fifth century and can tell you this is so. Even as you stand next to him on this adventure, he has already died. To change history is not your decision to make, though even an IntelliBoard can appreciate the compassion that you bring to the decision-making. (Fizzbin)

"Fizzbin says we go after the dragon," Dawk said. "So we go after the dragon."

CHAPTER

16

Dawk led Hype and Pliny through the back halls, away from the bustle, and he didn't mention one word of the conversation he had had with Fizzbin about Pliny's future.

"So, Fizzbin thinks you're still connected, it's just your brain doesn't know it," Dawk told his sister.

"Why doesn't it know it?" Hype asked.

"He says it's like your brain forgot your bypass existed, so it can't acknowledge it and connect with the temporal pathway."

"But how and why would that happen?"

Please inform Hype that scans through higher levels of the Alvarium banks have found information on NeuroNet overrides and disruptions in the research banks, which leads me to believe that these are of interest to the Ruling Cluster in the Alvarium. I'm not trying to suggest that the Ruling Cluster or any secret research labs have fiddled with Hype's neural bypass, but it is interesting that such things are being experimented with. I predict within a century, interrupting or even jamming a personal NeuroNet connection will be easy to do. (Fizzbin)

I don't know how to inform Hype of that. I don't really know what you just said. It sounded like a conspiracy theory. (Dawk)

Just tell her I'm working on it. (Fizzbin)

"Fizzbin says he's working on it and he has a few ideas," Dawk said.

"You have the most interesting conversations," Pliny said. "Is this Fizzbin that you continually mention a muse of some sort? Or perhaps it is a genie?"

Genie would be the best choice in this situation. (Fizzbin)

"Completely a genie," said Dawk.

"How fortunate you are to have a guardian spirit in your service," Pliny said.

"If you say so," Dawk said. "I find it a little irritating."

The group kept moving. As near as Dawk could tell, they were actually moving in the direction of the dragon, even though Hype kept saying nothing looked like the way she came in. Dawk tried to explain the concept of secret passages and that the CartoMod he was currently trapped in was more reliable than her memory, but then decided that they had chattered on enough and just needed to move.

He had no idea what they were going to do when they got to the dragon. No one had proper shielding, except for the OpBot, and that tiny thing was in no position to wrangle with a dragon.

They just kept moving. No plan. Dawk tried to accept that they were making it all up as they went along—or as quickly as Fizzbin could think of something.

"Stop, girl!" came a voice. "I'm parched!"

It was Antevorta, who must have slipped in

through a secret entrance. "I thought that my pouring girl was taking a good bit longer than she should," Antevorta said. "That is very disappointing, since this entire exercise was meant to create efficiency."

Antevorta stood still with a look of concentration. Dawk noticed the OpBot creeping behind her, and then felt a disruption in the Link—like it blinked off for a second, and then it returned.

What just happened? (Dawk)

That was a NackAttack. (Fizzbin)

A what? (Dawk)

A Negative Acknowledgement of Pathway Hack by way of an outside source. One of the points of research I found. Something tried to disrupt the Link. (Fizzbin)

And it didn't work? (Dawk)

You can still access me, though I know it irritates you. I'm collecting data. (Fizzbin)

"I'm sorry, I got a little distracted," Hype said.

Antevorta smiled. "Hypatia, I think you need to come with me and let history unfold," she said. "Enough of this flitting around dangerously with your comrades. Please, everyone, come with me.

Enjoy a refreshment. Learn how your world is to become."

There are readings emanating from this goddess that I can't make sense of. I'm picking up temporal event residue, as well as a controlled hum of electromagnetic energy not accounted for by your visual cortex filters. (Fizzbin)

Pliny stepped forward and faced Antevorta directly. "It seems unusual to me that a goddess of your position would sully herself with this business," he said, smiling. "Conquest and imperial takeovers and bloody power kerfuffles! Come, let us talk this over and decide what is better achieved through your immortal skill."

Pliny moved his face closer to Antevorta's, attempting to look her closely in the eyes, but Dawk could have sworn that her entire being flickered. She was confusing Pliny, he could see that.

"Your radiance fights to be sustained," Pliny said.

Antevorta staggered backward for a moment, as if she was dizzy. Suddenly, spasms in her back and neck seemed to cause her body to jolt slightly.

She looked at Hype. "I knew you were coming, Hypatia," she said. "That's why I kept you down here."

What's wrong with her? (Dawk)

The OpBot is wrong with her. It's giving her a jolt of electromagnetism to counteract her own field. (Fizzbin)

Dawk saw that the OpBot had affixed itself to her arm. It clung tight as she fell to her knees.

Regrettably, this will be my second OpBot fried on this mission, but it will be a worthwhile sacrifice. (Fizzbin)

It's pathetic when a goddess doesn't notice a little metal bug. (Dawk)

Divinity isn't all it's cracked up to be, Dawk. (Fizzbin)

Hype moved closer to Antevorta, who had begun flickering more noticeably. Her skin and her clothing began to have the appearance of a projection with a fading and transparent quality.

"Can I get you something?" Hype asked. She held up the jug she had been clutching. "I have this water. Would a sip help?"

Antevorta began laughing, and then laughed louder and harder. Then it seemed more like giggling. Finally, she went dark, and Dawk could no longer make out any of her features. She was no longer the goddess Antevorta, but a figure covered from head to toe in a visual cortex shell far more advanced than the ones Dawk and Hype wore.

The OpBot, now visible, dropped off her arm and landed with a clunk on the ground.

"We don't bother with OpBots anymore," Antevorta said, laughing. "Cybernetic clutter. I never even thought to consider one. Never even paid attention to the telltale readings. What an idiot."

"Who are you?" asked Hype.

"I'm Antevorta," the person in the suit said. "And events have already been set in motion. You can stop me, but you can't stop Domitian. And he's only one of many projects we have."

Antevorta had a small box in her hand that Dawk immediately recognized, a little gadget that he and Hype had first encountered in their visit to Prague. It was designed as a quick and simple temporal transporter—a couple finger gestures and you were time traveling. And it wasn't from the present—at least, not from Dawk and Hype's present.

It was from their future.

"Stop her!" Dawk yelled. He ran toward her, but then he felt a brief burst of energy and she disappeared into the air.

"I'm afraid I don't understand one thing that has happened here," Pliny said.

"Nothing to understand," Hype said. "The plan hasn't changed one bit. It's just gotten more important. We have to stop the dragon."

CHAPTER

17

It was hard to run while using a CartoMod, but Dawk went through the passages as fast as he could. Hype and Pliny were directly behind him.

"We're getting close!" Dawk said. "But I don't know what we're supposed to do when we get there!"

"We stop the dragon," said Hype, but even she wasn't sure how they were going to do that.

Dawk, you must explain to Hype the nature of the dragon. That information is crucial to containing it. (Fizzbin)

I don't know what to tell her. (Dawk)

You may refer to it as a biological robot, the result of a very advanced technology that is able to place information into DNA strands like you would a computer chip. The tissue then must build on itself to understand its organic programming. (Fizzbin)

You mean in the future they grow flesh robots? (Dawk)

I shudder to think about it. (Fizzbin)

As they ran through the maze of the Hypogeum corridors, Dawk did his best to explain to Hype what Fizzbin had just told him, only without using Fizzbin's vocabulary. Hype trotted along beside him, absorbing all of the complicated information. Pliny didn't speak, but Dawk could tell he was listening, fascinated.

"There, ahead!" Hype yelled. She recognized the passage to the dragon's lair and moved quickly ahead of Dawk to reach it.

When she ripped open the door, they saw something no one expected. The dragon was currently muzzled and being handled by four guards. Each guard guided the creature using a pole that was connected to a chain and shackle on each of its legs. The sight of the people at the door made the guards stop.

Then, with a puffed-out chest, Pliny pushed his way in front of Hype.

"I need to inspect the creature before launch," Pliny said.

I had no idea he was such a quick thinker. (Dawk)

Neither did I. (Fizzbin)

"Her luminosity had previously ordered that —" one of the men began.

"Do you really expect the dragon to do what it must without a clean bill of health?" Pliny snapped. "We only get one chance at this operation, and if the dragon fails, it's all over!"

"But Domitian said—"

"I am the foremost expert on dragons in the entire Empire, and it was Domitian himself who asked me to examine the beast! When it cannot perform its fiery duties above the skies of Rome, I will have Domitian come to you personally and ask you for an explanation."

"But surely that can only be a good thing, since it ensures that Domitian will—"

"I thought you were a loyalist!" Pliny screeched. "You question Domitian?"

The guard sighed and motioned to his comrades to stand still. Pliny walked up and began poking at the dragon's torso. The dragon seemed irritated by it, but the muzzle guaranteed Pliny was safe from a burst of fire breath.

"His flame bags feel firm," Pliny said. "We need to check his mid-wing rotors."

"I'll do that," Hype volunteered. She climbed onto the dragon's back.

"Good. Now we need to get his wings moving slightly while you feel the rotor movement."

Pliny began to tickle the dragon slightly on its backside, and its wings did begin to slowly register the sensation. The soldiers held their poles firm.

"It feels okay," Hype said, "but I'm a little concerned at how things will be handled at maximum velocity."

"Then perhaps we need to find out," Pliny said. He took off his shoe and gave the dragon a whack on its rear end. The animal turned around quickly, snapping at the old man beneath its muzzle. It was upset. The wings were still moving slowly, though. Hype kicked it, as though it were a horse.

That did the trick. The fury of the beast was so incredible that the guards, no matter how hard they tried, could not keep hold of the shackles. Once the dragon found itself free, the guards ran, and Dawk and Pliny followed. The dragon whipped around in a rage and Hype kicked it one more time to make sure there were no mistakes. The dragon took a frenzied running leap and dove into the air, shooting down the dark path and out of the sight of the onlookers in moments.

"Well, I'd say that's a very healthy dragon, wouldn't you?" Pliny said. He smiled.

CHAPTER

18

Hype took a deep breath, opened her eyes, and kept clinging to the strap of the dragon's muzzle.

It was really happening. She was riding a dragon.

The dragon was so graceful. Where had this creature come from?

She closed her eyes again, but this time not out of shock or fear of what was to come. This time, it was to enjoy the wind in her hair and the movement of the dragon. It was to enjoy being in the moment, something she felt she rarely had a chance to do.

Surely there was no reason this had to end.

❀

The Hypogeum was in chaos as Dawk and Pliny ran through it, pushing people out of the way. They were trying to get above ground to find Hype and the dragon. Quite a few of the people down below wanted to get up as well, but guards were loudly warning the crowds that they were safer down there. Domitian would be facing off with the dragon, and though the guards had every confidence in his victory over the beast, they also knew it would be a hard-fought one. There was potential for damage and injury to anything or anyone that happened to be nearby.

This is all going to have to be accomplished with an OpBot. (Fizzbin)

I know. (Dawk)

I could have Benton send another OpBot back, but schedule it for an hour ago, so that it was already around to track Hype. (Fizzbin)

We know where Hype is headed. Here. (Dawk)

Dawk continued fleeing to the ramp with Pliny.

Once they reached it, Pliny climbed up first, so it was Dawk's responsibility to not only get himself up, but to help the old man in front of him.

Dawk pushed. And pushed. And pushed. He was physically prepared, but this was proving difficult. Pliny clung to the edges and was able to help Dawk help him.

Before long, Pliny was at the top. He crawled into the Colosseum, Dawk behind him. They dashed back to the outer wall and past the guard, hurriedly looking around and trying to figure out where to go.

That was when they ran into Dawk's parents.

"Dawk!" said Mom. "Where is your sister? The city is in a panic!"

"Um, she's around somewhere," Dawk said.

She's busy putting her overnight observations on a scroll for Pliny. No bull monsters, but plenty of moths to record. (Fizzbin)

"Vespasian just walked out on a consult with us," Dad said, rolling his eyes. "We were so close to finally getting him to open up about personal footwear for senators, despite his feelings about the military versions, when an attendant interrupted. Something about a dragon."

"Attacking!" said Mom. "A dragon! In Rome! Whoever heard of such a thing? It's probably some oversized hawk flying around that's got everyone upset!"

"Would you happen to know where the Emperor's son Domitian is stationed currently?" asked Pliny.

"You must be Pliny! So nice to meet you!" said Dad.

"We've heard so much about you—from Dawk and Hype, of course, and then—well, other sources," Mom said.

At that moment, Titus came running up and grabbed Pliny.

"You must join me at the Temple of Jupiter on Capitoline Hill, where Domitian stands on top, waiting," Titus said. "My brother has been visited by a goddess, and he is to face off against a dragon in defense of Rome! No doubt the dragon that's ravaging the countryside as we speak!"

"Are you to fight with him?" Pliny asked.

"No, only the bearer of the sword and shield provided by the goddess Antevorta can stand against the serpent!" Titus said. "I am not allowed by that decree. Domitian is destined to be savior of the Empire. We must help him!"

Titus ran and Pliny followed. Dawk took off after Pliny. His parents were right behind him.

Well, this is terribly symbolic. The Temple of Jupiter is one the most important places in Ancient Rome, built on the site where it is believed Rome itself was founded by the mythical Romulus. Defeating the dragon here would enlarge the meaning of that victory for the Roman people. Domitian would be like a god to them. Marrying Antevorta and conquering Olympus would be a small leap from there. (Fizzbin)

It's a good thing I don't think history is going to unfold the way Domitian wants. (Dawk)

Dawk was glad that dealing with the dragon was mostly Hype's problem, since trying to burst through the crowds with any speed was almost impossible. The chaos was created by a ferocious mix of the fearful fleeing the battle and the curious clamoring to get there in time. A giant swirl of people were clogging up the center of Rome. Even with Titus in the lead, their movement was slow. Everyone was too frenzied to take notice of the Emperor's son.

It was a slow slog. On a normal day, it would have taken a third of the time to get to Capitoline Hill, but once they did and started moving upward, everyone could see Domitian. He was standing and looking to the west, sword and shield in hand.

Titus moved forward and everyone in their little party followed. Other Romans also moved in the same direction.

"I am ready for you, Ladon!" Domitian yelled into the horizon. "We thought you dead, but you have returned! You shall not bring destruction to Rome!" He swiped his sword in the air again a couple of times to amplify his threat.

"What is that man raving about?" Dad asked, staring at Domitian.

"He seems a little nutty," Dawk said.

He is claiming that the dragon is Ladon, who guarded a tree of golden apples and was disposed of by the man-god Hercules. The dragon was sent into the sky by the goddess Hera, Jupiter's wife. Domitian certainly knows what he is doing when it comes to the art of manipulation. (Fizzbin)

Dad eyed Dawk suspiciously. "You and your sister don't have anything to do with this, do you?" he asked.

"We've never seen a dragon in our lives, Dad," Dawk said. He smiled. Then he turned back to the action and watched as Pliny and Titus approached Domitian.

"Are you sure you are prepared for a dragon, especially one as legendary for nastiness as Ladon?" Pliny asked.

"Both of you stand aside," Domitian said with a sneer. "Rome has me to protect it."

"Of course it does," Pliny said, bowing. "Forgive us."

Dawk crept closer. Soon, he was standing just behind Pliny.

"I have been fearful that my brother might be mad, jealous as I know he is of my military history," Titus whispered to Pliny. "But with his presentation of such a fine sword and shield to match, and his sincerity at the story, I want to ignore my worst thoughts on the matter. Should I?"

"All that remains for us is to wait and see," Pliny advised him.

And that wasn't to be long. The dragon was in the distance. It was flying straight toward the Temple of Jupiter. The crowd gasped at the sight. Domitian steadied his stance.

The dragon kept moving forward.

CHAPTER
19

It seemed to Hype that the dragon was on autopilot, like her place on its back didn't make any difference in its destination. That's something she should have guessed would happen, but she was so taken by the sensation of riding the dragon's back that she hadn't given much thought to how to control it.

Even with Hype along for the ride, and even with the muzzle, the dragon would surely still attack Domitian like it was supposed to.

She didn't know what to do. Without NeuroPedia

access, there wasn't even a possibility that she could come up with a solution. What did she know about dragons? They were fictional, after all.

All she had was whatever info was in her NeuroCache. She quickly opened access and began to scan through the debris there. Most of it was nonsense about PlayMods and such that she had no use for.

There had to be something in there.

She had forgotten that part of the clutter was the scenario data for Draggin' Dragons. That wasn't much to go on, but it was the only thing she had. PlayMods were often based on real historical or biological facts, after all.

Hype scanned through the information, trying to figure out what the best possible outcome would be. She definitely didn't want the dragon to blow up, not while she was on it. She was looking for something physical, something that would help her situation. Maybe there was something in the game that was applicable to the dragon she was on right that moment, something that would translate from a PlayMod on NeuroNet to actual, real life.

She could see Domitian in the distance. They were getting closer and closer.

Hype scanned further and more frantically into her cache. She stumbled onto information about a higher playing level that existed in the PlayMod in which the player had the opportunity to overtake the Draggin' Dragon, actually ride its back, and use it to fight other Draggin' Dragons. There had to be some sort of controls on the Draggin' Dragon to do that.

Directionals!

She could change the trajectory of the flight by using the dragon's directionals. Did real dragons have directionals like PlayMod dragons?

Hype took a leap of faith and let the cached scenario data take over and fill her with the PlayMod player's instinct. She put her hand down on the dragon's spine. She felt a point of contact that was hard to describe. It was a physical sensation without anything physically noticeable about the surface of the dragon. She moved her hand one way and the dragon slowed down.

Domitian would at least have an extra moment

to think about his defense unless she shifted to other controller gestures.

She tapped the dragon on the central point of contact, and the creature went limp.

Hype and the dragon were plummeting from the sky.

So real dragons were similar to PlayMod dragons. What were the odds?

On the ground, at the temple, the crowd of people screamed.

"Is that Hype on the dragon?" asked Mom.

Dawk did not want to answer.

The dragon continued its nosedive.

Then Hype remembered something the guards in the dark cave had said when the dragon had gone limp. "The igniter is in the spine."

She brought her hand down on the spine,

pressing firm. It was just the matter of a reboot, really.

She felt energy in the dragon's body, which then took flight upward. The jolt of the sudden change in direction almost threw her off, but she held tight with one hand, and began experimenting with the controller again.

Up.

Left.

Right.

Up.

Down.

Up.

Down.

⊙◎ ❖ ◎⊙

"It is Hype!" screamed Mom. "And she's doing loop-de-loops."

Dawk laughed. Pliny laughed. Soon, everyone was laughing, while Domitian stared at the young girl on the dragon spinning around in the sky. Her own screams and giggles echoed out to the crowds.

"I've saved you, Rome, you're safe now!" she screamed and did some more loop-de-loops. The citizens of Rome screamed and cheered and ignored Domitian altogether.

CHAPTER 20

By the next day, the excitement had died down. It was quiet so suddenly, it was almost as if everyone was ordered to calm down. On the way to Pliny's that morning, it seemed like business as usual in the streets of Rome.

Dawk and Hype were organizing the scrolls about dragons scattered around Pliny's study when they heard someone enter the main room. The two tiptoed over and hunched next to the doorway. It was Titus, and he sounded cautious—not friendly like he usually was.

The day before, everyone had watched as Titus calmed down Domitian enough so he could leave the site of the so-called dragon attack with a military escort. It was in front of the entire city of Rome, which must have been pretty embarrassing for the Emperor and Domitian.

"As your patron, I need to ask one favor of you," Titus said. "It is imperative that this incident with the dragon not be mentioned in your encyclopedia. I have also seen that the incident is expunged from all city records. I confess it is entirely to spare my brother's ego, but even you must admit that it is probably in the best interests of the Empire."

"Do you think Pliny will tell him what a creep his brother is?" Dawk whispered to his sister.

"I'll bet he keeps it to himself for now," Hype said. "Until he really needs to."

"Besides, all is not lost," Titus said to Pliny. "I do have some interesting ideas about the Colosseum. I see how bravery against beasts unites the Roman citizenry. I'm sure there is a way to replicate that for a nation's sake."

Dawk and Hype had looked at NeuroPedia.

They knew the Colosseum would have a bloody future—or history, to them. It would soon become a place of violent battles between people and animals, and the Hypogeum would be a major part.

But Pliny had different ideas and, after Titus left, he told Dawk and Hype all about these plans. He would soon be off on his prefecture with the Navy, but he was looking further on, applying what he had learned and how it could benefit his life's work: knowledge.

"When I come back, I plan to tackle the issue of the Hypogeum myself," he told them. "It would make a wonderful place to keep animal specimens and do research on nature. A menagerie of learning! I feel that since it was created in secret, I can convince my lord Titus of the favor, especially given what I have agreed to do for him this day. And after facing a dragon, I feel I am prepared to face any furious force of nature that exists, including the Emperor's son."

There was only one thing about the whole event that still seemed to nag at Pliny.

"You say that you just let the dragon go?" he

asked Hype. "To fly free and put more civilizations in peril?"

"When I was on its back, flying, I knew it was a creature that deserved to be free in all its glory," Hype said. "It's not good or bad. It just is."

Pliny had sympathy for a feisty flying creature being chained down by civilization, so he accepted Hype's answer.

But it wasn't the truth.

Once Hype had finished showing off for everybody in Rome—with a special triple swirl for Emperor Vespasian, who had finally shown up—Hype had figured out the controller enough to guide the dragon out of the city and back near the cave that it used as a hangar. When she got there, she circled it around. She eased it into landing. And then she put it to sleep.

As she stood by, four people—three women and a man—materialized and began webbing the dragon with some temporal sensors. One of them gave a thumbs-up to Hype, and a moment later, they—along with the dragon—were gone.

She assumed Fizzbin had alerted Benton and

they had calculated the location. But Hype didn't really know for sure. And she didn't even know where the dragon was being taken. She was sure it would never fly again. The technology that had created the dragon was eras ahead of the twenty-fifth century. It was going to be in a lab somewhere, isolated from everything.

CHAPTER 21

And so Rome fell into a peaceful calm.

From what Dawk and Hype had noticed, many of the guards they had seen down in the Hypogeum—either Domitian loyalists or perhaps the husbands of pushy Antevorta worshippers—were now above ground, apparently back to their pre-Antevorta posts. They would have another chance to be on a new Emperor's side in a few years. Everything seemed to be back to normal.

Mom and Dad had a couple more weeks to tie up their work before the family moved on, so

Dawk and Hype had more time to help Pliny. That made them happy. With the new OpBot spinning along beside them, each day they made their way to Pliny's living space and spent the day helping him catalog further—though dragon hunting was no longer on the table.

"I don't mind being off-Link, actually," Hype said one morning as they strolled through Rome. "It's peaceful. And after my experience, hearing everyone go on about Draggin' Dragons would just make me roll my eyes. After we get back, I think I might wait to have my adjustments done until the next big PlayMod comes along."

She was quiet for another moment. "I do know what is going to happen to Pliny after he goes off with the Navy," she said. "I checked him out on NeuroPedia after we met him."

"If we had let Domitian take over Rome, it might have saved his life," Dawk said.

"Time unfolds the way it unfolds, and we don't have any right to mess around with that," Hype said, shaking her head. "Besides, if I understand correctly what's going on, it seems like there are people out there—time travelers, probably—who are trying to change time. I don't know why, but they're interfering for some reason. I think we're supposed to be stopping that from happening, not making it happen, right?"

Dawk shrugged. "I guess so," he said. "I mean, I think."

"I've also been thinking about Draggin' Dragons," Hype said. "Remember when I got sucked into that PlayMod? It couldn't have been coincidental. It was like a secret message from the future contained in a PlayMod, wasn't it? That dragon had the same controller as the PlayMod version. That's no accident!"

"Who would go to all that trouble to send you a secret message?" asked Dawk. "And how would they know you were going to be here, in Ancient Rome, riding a dragon?"

"Because they live in the future, so they know what happened in the past. Use your brain. Or just ask Fizzbin."

What do you think, Fizzbin? (Dawk)

I have several theories, but I don't wish to confuse the

two of you with anything too complicated. I suggest you make up your own stories. (Fizzbin)

Well, that's only a little bit insulting. (Dawk)

Please don't claim I didn't warn you. One idea I have is that the PlayMod makers are from our future and they traveled to the past to create Draggin' Dragons and pull Hype into it. (Fizzbin)

But why would they do that? (Dawk)

Forget that one, then. Perhaps Draggin' Dragons is the result of some cross-temporal vReality development. It is the next step after the cross-temporal NeuroNet access that you enjoy, after all. You have a server in one time, but it is accessed in another time. (Fizzbin)

So that people from different times can enter the same PlayMod? (Dawk)

Exactly! Imagine how challenging it would be to compete against the different skill sets of various eras in history! (Fizzbin)

Got any other theories? (Dawk)

Of course. Consider the idea that time is an unstructured force that our own minds give form to through our processing, as we do with light waves and audio frequencies. We only think of it as linear and contained because our brains tell us to. Take away that brain function and reality as we see it breaks down. The laws of physics will bend. You could use the same principal to have a PlayMod exist in two eras. Digital temporality. Simple, no? (Fizzbin)

No. You're confusing me. A lot. (Dawk)

"So does Fizzbin have any ideas?" Hype asked.

"None that I can explain to you without a degree in advanced physics, or at least an active imagination," Dawk told his sister. "I just hope we don't meet up with these people on our next trip through time. This is exhausting."

CHAPTER 22

When they arrived at Pliny's, the old man was busily looking through some scrolls and nodding as he read. "Ah! Just in time for the Blemmyes!" he said.

"Is that some kind of sickness?" Hype asked.

"Or a new olive-based snack that you just invented?" Dawk said.

"What is the most horrifying vision you can imagine?" Pliny asked.

"A new olive-based snack that you just invented," Dawk admitted.

"How about the headless?" Pliny asked.

"The headless what?" Hype asked.

"The headless who roam the earth!"

Here he goes again. (Fizzbin)

"It is said that there is a race to the south that has no heads above their shoulders," Pliny said. "A peaceful group, by some accounts, but horrifying to witness. Their eyes are on their shoulders, their mouths near their bellies, their brains embedded in the creatures' chests. And yet they do resemble human beings with the appropriate corresponding limbs."

"Have you seen them?" asked Hype.

"No, but I hope to," Pliny said. "After my tour with the Navy, I will have them leave me in Africa before returning to Rome. I'm not one to take expeditions of discovery, but the Blemmyes, I think, are reason to ignore that tendency."

"What would you do if you got to meet them?" Dawk asked.

"Try to communicate with them, of course!" Pliny said. "For instance, if their brains are encased in ribs, is it possible these obstruct the effects of the moon and madness does not exist for this race? Such fascinating possibilities!"

"Do you really believe in these things?" Dawk asked.

"Just yesterday, I saw a mechanical dragon made out of flesh being flown by a young girl who speaks to her brother with her mind," Pliny said. "I see nothing farfetched about the Blemmyes or any other strange thing you can think of."

He held out a bowl to the two time travelers. "Please! Have an olive before we get to work."

Dawk politely refused.

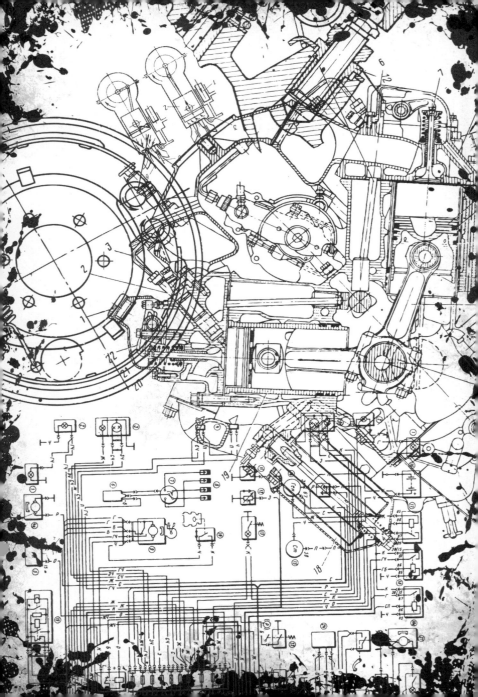

ABOUT THE AUTHOR

John Seven grew up in the 1970s, when science fiction movies and TV shows were cheap and fun. His favorites shows were *The Starlost, Land of the Lost,* and *Return to the Planet of the Apes,* and he loved time travel most of all. John collaborated with his wife, illustrator Jana Christy, on the comic book *Very Vicky* and a number of children's books, including *A Year With Friends, A Rule Is To Break: A Child's Guide To Anarchy, Happy Punks 1-2-3,* and the multi-award-winning *The Ocean Story.* John was born in Savannah, Georgia, and currently lives in North Adams, Massachussetts, with his wife and their twin sons, Harry and Hugo, where they all watch a lot of *Doctor Who* and *Lost* together.

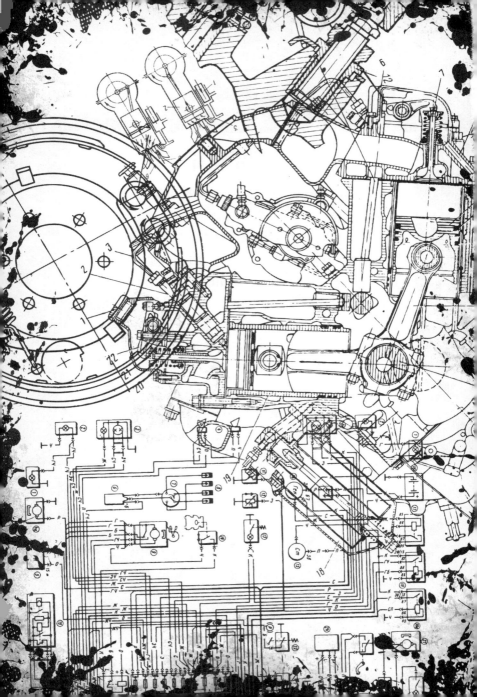